DATE DUE			
GAYLORD			PRINTED IN U.S.A.

STOLEN BY THE SEA

ALSO BY ANNA MYERS

Stolen by the Sea

Anna Myers

WALKER & COMPANY
NEW YORK

First published in the United States of America in 2002 by
Walker Publishing Company, Inc.

Published simultaneously in Canada by
Fitzhenry and Whiteside, Markham, Ontario L3R 4T8

Library of Congress Cataloging-in-Publication Data
Myers, Anna.
Stolen by the sea / Anna Myers.
p.   cm.
Summary: In Galveston, Texas, a rich twelve-year-old girl and
an orphaned fourteen-year-old boy work together to save
themselves and others from the terrible hurricane of 1900.
ISBN 0-8027-8787-8
1. Hurricanes—Texas—Galveston—Juvenile fiction.
[1. Hurricanes—Texas—Galveston—Fiction.   2. Survival—
Fiction.   3. Orphans—Fiction.   4. Friendship—Fiction.
5. Mexican Americans—Fiction.   6. Galveston (Tex.)—
Fiction.]   I. Title.
PZ7.M9814 St 2001
[Fic]—dc21 2001026157

Book design by Jennifer Ann Daddio

Printed in the United States of America

2 4 6 8 10 9 7 5 3 1

This book is dedicated with love to four old friends
who helped me with it.

First, to John Calvin, who came from my long-ago high
school days to pull me back into the world and to be
an invaluable help with the storm research.

Next, to my always dear friends from college: Tom Sims, who
drove me to Galveston and helped me have fun again, and,
of course, Beverly and Bob McBride, who shared their
beautiful old Galveston home with me and
taught me to love their city.

The book is also dedicated to the memory of my husband,
who had begun a story about the hurricane. This is our
book, Paul, and I too have survived the storm.

STOLEN BY THE SEA

ONE

BEFORE THE STORM, Maggie McKenna lived in a big
house, tall and white. Inside it smelled of furniture polish
and the roses from Mama's garden. Upstairs in her bedroom,
Maggie had new dresses with lace and starched collars. On
her bed were a pink organdy spread and big soft pillows.

Before the storm Maggie's house stood on the corner of a
wide street lined with huge oak trees. Around the house was
a sparkling white fence that separated Maggie's house from
her city. Maggie loved her city. She loved Galveston, Texas.
Maggie's papa called Galveston the Queen of the Gulf. Galveston had sturdy brick buildings, theaters, and flowers. Best of
all, Galveston had the sea with its crashing blue-green waves
or its peaceful lapping sound. Maggie loved to walk on the
beach with her collie dog, Bonnie, and she loved to run into
the water with her friends, Beth and Harriet. Papa taught all

three girls to swim in the gulf, and on summer evenings he often took them to enjoy a dip. Before the storm Maggie loved the sea.

The storm came in September, but all that summer Maggie felt a storm building inside her, a dark storm caused by jealousy. "Don't be so hateful," she would whisper to herself when she felt the storm rumbling inside her. She would shake her head and try to smile, but the darkness would not be driven out. Maggie's father liked boys best. She knew that with a terrible certainty, knew it whenever she saw Papa with Felipe, who came from the orphanage to work in the garden.

"What a fine knife," Papa said to Felipe one day in early July. Maggie had just carried Felipe a sandwich to eat for lunch and a big glass of lemonade. Mama always liked to make sure Felipe ate well when he worked through lunchtime. He laid down the knife he had just used to cut string to tie up a rosebush.

Maggie saw her papa coming up the walk and ran to meet him. He put his arm around her shoulder, and they walked together to the back steps. There Papa stopped and spoke to Felipe. He also looked down at the knife. "That's a fine knife," Papa said.

"It belonged to my *tata*." Felipe stroked the knife that lay beside him. "It is all that I have of his. My *tata* could carve from wood, beautiful things. I am trying to learn."

Papa put his hand on Felipe's shoulder. "I enjoy carving too," he said, "although I am no great artist. Maybe we could work together sometimes."

Felipe looked up at Papa, and Maggie saw how his eyes sparkled. "That would be very nice," he said.

"I am sure your father was proud to have a son like you," Papa said. "Any man would be proud."

Papa's arm was still around Maggie's shoulder, but she wiggled away and went on inside. Tears burned at her eyes. "Don't cry," she told herself. She knew she shouldn't. Hadn't Papa told her just recently that he was proud of her? Couldn't she share her papa a little with an orphan like Felipe? She went often to the orphanage with her mama. Mama liked to help there with the sewing for the children, and Maggie liked going. She never minded when Mama lifted a lonely child to her lap. Maggie did not mind sharing Mama, but Papa was different. Mama did not like boys best.

She had known that Papa liked boys best for several months now, since not long after Felipe came to work for them. "Perhaps we should consider taking in one of the boys over at St. Mary's," Papa said to Mama. Maggie had sat quietly on the front porch swing, and she heard the conversation through the parlor window.

"Oh, no, Charles." Mama's voice sounded horrified. "The child would not be a true McKenna. I know I will give you a son. Just be patient."

"It isn't the blood that matters, Katherine," Papa said. "Look at young Felipe. He is dear to me already. Perhaps we should adopt him."

"Charles! What a strange idea. The boy is practically grown. He's far too old. I can't take some boy who is almost a man into my home. And what about his little sisters? He wouldn't want to leave them at the orphanage. Besides, there's Maggie. She could never adjust to suddenly having a half-grown brother."

Maggie had slipped off the swing then and made her way quietly down the stairs. Felipe was working in the back garden, pulling the tiny pieces of grass that kept trying to come up in the flower beds. His dark head was bent over the flower beds, and he could not see Maggie watching him. He sang as he worked, but the words were ones he had learned in Mexico before he came to Galveston with his mother and father. Maggie could not understand his song.

"Sing in English," she said to him. Then she lied to the boy her father wanted for a son. "Papa said you should always speak English here."

Felipe raised his head, but he did not turn toward Maggie. "I was not speaking to you," he said. "I was singing to myself and to the flowers."

"It is silly to sing to flowers," Maggie said. "How old are you?"

"I am thirteen years."

"That's older than I am," she said. "Thirteen is too old to be adopted!" Maggie's words came out as a shout.

"I do not plan to be adopted," Felipe said quietly. "When my birthday comes next year I will leave St. Mary's. The sisters there are good, but an orphanage is no place for a four-teen-year-old."

"Where will you go?" She did not shout this time. She

could see that Felipe would not tolerate much shouting. If she wanted to talk to him, she could not speak in anger.

This time he turned to look at Maggie before he spoke. "What do you care where it is that I go?"

Maggie shrugged her shoulders. "Just wondered."

Felipe pointed. "That way," he said. "I will go back to Mexico, and I will find my *abuelos.*"

"*Abuelos?* What does that mean? Speak English."

"Grandparents," Felipe said, and he bent back over the flower beds. "I will go home and find my *abuelos.*"

"You will leave your little sisters in the orphanage?" Maggie asked. Maggie had often seen Felipe at the orphanage with his twin sisters. She liked him then, forgetting how jealous she felt when her papa stopped to talk to him even before he came into the house to say hello to her and Mama. Felipe was good to the little girls, who seemed always to be following him.

"I have two little shadows," she had heard him say. He laughed and hugged the little girls to him. Maggie had liked his laugh at the orphanage, but now she felt too jealous to like anything about him.

He did not answer her question, so she asked again. "What about your little sisters?"

"I will return for my little sisters," he said, and he went back to pulling weeds. Maggie could see that the conversation was over. She would be glad when Felipe left for Mexico. Let him find his own family and leave hers alone.

But that had been a few months ago, before anyone knew

there would be a baby. Mama and Papa did not talk to Maggie about the baby because they thought she was too young to know about such things, but Maggie knew. "If God is merciful," Maggie had heard Mama tell Aunt Susan when she had come from Houston to visit, "I'll carry this child until December."

Maggie wished Mama and Papa didn't think she was too young to talk to about the baby and too young to know about the others, the babies that had come too soon to live. Maggie knew. She knew why Mama had stayed in bed crying and Papa's face had looked gray and sad.

In late July Maggie celebrated her birthday. After dinner that night, Harriet came from across the street, and Beth came from across town. The two girls walked up the front walk together, and Maggie watched them from the doorway. She felt lucky to have such good friends. They were nothing alike. Beth was blond, like Maggie herself, and she laughed almost all the time. Harriet had dark hair and eyes. She did not have to fear the Galveston sun as much as her fair-skinned friends did. Harriet did not laugh as much as Beth, but she never missed anything. Maggie had never told either girl how she felt about her papa wanting a boy, but she was pretty sure Harriet knew.

Both girls carried gifts wrapped in bright paper, and Maggie opened them as soon as her friends were inside. Beth's gift was a book full of clean white paper for drawing. Harriet brought a necklace, a small white heart painted with roses.

"Thank you," Maggie said as she opened each gift, and

she said thank you again before her attention turned to the table with her cake. Mama felt tired, so she sat with her feet up on the settee beside her. She took a small box from beneath a pillow and held it out to Maggie.

"This is from your papa and me," she said. Mama gave Maggie a hug when Maggie bent down to take the gift.

The box held a beautiful pearl ring. "Oh!" said Maggie. "Oh!"

"You are a young lady now," Mama said. "Twelve is old enough to wear a real pearl ring."

"Yes," Papa said. "You are a beautiful, grown-up young lady."

Suddenly Maggie wished the ring had been a doll. She wanted to shout out that she did not want to be grown up. She looked over at her birthday cake on the table. Papa started to light the candles. Maggie wanted to shout something else too. She wanted to yell that she did not want her father to have a son either. She knew for sure that if the baby Mama would have in December turned out to be a boy, everyone would forget all about her.

"The candles are ready," Papa said.

"Don't forget to make a wish," Harriet said.

"And blow out all the candles at once. That way your wish will come true," Beth told her.

Maggie closed her eyes. I wish the baby would be born too soon, she thought. Then she stopped. How could she wish such a thing? How could she want a baby not to have life? How could she want her mama and papa to be so sad?

Shame spread through her like heat from a fireplace. What could she do to take back her wish? She could fail to blow out the candles. She opened her eyes and blew gently. Only two candles went out.

"Well," she said, "I guess that wish won't come true." She blew out the other ten candles at once.

"What did you wish?" Beth asked.

Maggie looked down at the cake and thought quickly. "I wished school wouldn't start in September. I wished we would have another month of vacation."

Beth had doubt on her face. "That's strange. You like school. That wasn't your real wish, was it?"

Maggie felt her face grow red.

"You don't have to tell us your wish," Harriet said. "On your birthday, you can have some secrets."

Maggie smiled at Harriet. She glanced at her parents. Good! They did not seem to be listening. Papa was busy cutting the cake and putting pieces on little plates. Mama had her eyes closed and her head back against a pillow.

It was the next day that she saw the dog Felipe had carved. It looked like Bonnie. Felipe had it in his hand when he knocked on the back door.

He made it for me, Maggie thought, and she felt ashamed of how angry she had felt toward Felipe. The dog was not perfect, but she could definitely tell that it was meant to be Bonnie. Maybe she and Felipe could get to be friends, Maggie thought.

Felipe saw her looking at the dog, and suddenly he

shoved it hard into his pocket. "It is not very good," he said. "Your father tried to help me, but I need more lessons."

Maggie forgot her warm feelings. Felipe had no intention of giving her the dog. It was not right for him to carve a likeness of *her* dog with *her* father. Now he wanted more lessons.

"Papa isn't here," she snapped. "Surely you know he is always at the bank on Monday mornings."

"I do know," said Felipe, and he backed down the steps.

Maggie closed the door and leaned against it. She wanted to cry, but Mama came into the kitchen just then. "Is something wrong?" Mama asked.

"Just Felipe." Maggie made a face. "He made a carving of Bonnie. I thought he meant to give it to me, but he didn't. Do you think he should be allowed to make carvings of my dog?"

Mama put out her hand to touch Maggie's blond hair. "Oh, sweetheart, your father told me about the carving. Felipe made it for your birthday. Probably he started to feel too shy to give it to you."

Maggie shook her head. She did not want to believe it. "I don't think so," she said, but she wasn't sure. Why couldn't things just be simple like they used to be? She took Mama's arm and leaned her face against it. "Mama," she said, "sometimes I am not a very good person." Tears slipped from her eyes and ran down her cheek. "I am going to try to be better."

"You are good," Mama said, "not perfect, but none of us are." She stopped to kiss Maggie's cheek. "I think you've grown up to be a fine lady."

"Mama." Maggie swallowed big. It was hard to talk to

Mama, but she felt determined. "Don't you think I'm grown up enough to talk to about why you are always sick?"

Mama looked at Maggie for a minute before she spoke. "I'm not sick, darling, not exactly, more just tired. It is a hot summer, but I will feel better. You are not to worry about me."

Mama hugged Maggie, who noticed that her mother's face seemed too white. What if having this baby was too much for Mama? Maggie had heard about lots of women who died giving birth. Would her papa be happy then? she wondered. Even if Mama died, would he be happy just to have a son?

All through July and August, Maggie worried. Mama seemed to have no strength at all. Often she did not leave her bed until just before the evening meal. Maggie felt lonely with Mama so often in bed. Harriet had gone away on a trip with her mother to visit relatives in Louisiana, and Beth was away at her grandmother's in Houston.

Only Myra seemed to have time for Maggie, and she often helped the housekeeper with her chores. Myra had worked for Papa's family since he was just a child not much older than Maggie. One morning Mama and Papa discussed Myra at breakfast.

"Charles, we have to have more help. Myra is just too old to manage this house anymore," Mama said.

"She keeps saying she won't have some silly woman getting in her way." Papa put his newspaper down on the breakfast table.

"Well, tell her you insist. After all, you are her employer.

Of course she will always have her room and her salary, but we have to have more help. Later, you know . . ." Mama moved her eyes in Maggie's direction. "Later we will need much more help. Just tell her, dear."

"I will, Katherine. I will," Papa said.

Maggie did not want someone else new in the house. Already there was a new cook, Daphne, who was hard to get along with. "I'll help Myra," she said. "Myra and I like to work together."

Mama smiled at her, but neither she nor Papa really seemed to hear what Maggie had said. They hardly know I'm here, she thought.

In the evenings Papa spent lots of time sitting beside Mama. Sometimes he read aloud to her. "Come and listen, why don't you?" Papa would call to Maggie, but she didn't.

It was a restless, unhappy summer for Maggie, but in late August she decided to go to the orphanage alone. She had never been there without Mama, and it made her feel grown up. On the long trolley ride, she looked out at Galveston. The city was full of bright flowers and busy people. I want to live here always, Maggie thought. There could be no other spot as wonderful as Galveston.

Maggie could see St. Mary's from where the trolley stopped. Two buildings stood on the grounds, tall and strong. They were made from brick and rock, and they were surrounded by a black iron fence.

Maggie did not go inside the fence right away. First, she wanted to look at the sea. Most of the time Maggie felt really sorry for the girls and boys who lived at St. Mary's because they didn't have a mama or papa or a regular house to live in, but when she looked at the sea, Maggie felt envious of the orphans. Maggie loved the great magical water better than just about anything. When the children of St. Mary's looked out the windows after they got up in the morning, they could see the ocean, and at night the waves would sing them to sleep.

She climbed the stairs to the brick building, and her stomach felt a little uneasy. Maybe it was silly for her to come here to help all by herself. Maybe she really was too young to do anything. At the door, she hesitated before she knocked, but then she drew in her breath and stood tall. The sisters would be glad to see her. They were, Maggie believed, the kindest people in the world.

"Is there a job I can do?" Maggie asked the sister who opened the door. "I'm Katherine McKenna's daughter. My mama is too sick to come to sew, but I would like to help somehow if I can."

"You could play with the little girls," said the sister. "It would make them very happy."

"It would make me happy too," said Maggie.

The sister went up the stairs and came back with a group of little girls, who were all about the same size. They ran eagerly to Maggie. "Where should we play?" Maggie asked the sister, and she was pointed toward a back door.

When Maggie had the girls settled on the back lawn, she had the chance to look at them. Felipe's little sisters, Rosa and

Maria, were there along with four other girls. "What should we play?" Maggie asked.

"Button, button, who has the button," yelled a little red-headed girl.

"That would be good. Let me think what we could use for a button." Maggie felt in her pocket for the nickel trolley fare she would use to get back home, but she was afraid the nickel might get lost in the grass.

"We could use Rosa's or Maria's necklace," suggested the same little girl.

The twins looked at each other, and their hands went to their throats. Each girl wore a small wooden cross fastened to a black ribbon. The crosses were made of red wood, and the finish shone in the afternoon sun.

Neither of the little girls said anything, but they looked at Maggie with distress. Maggie smiled at them. "I don't think Rosa or Maria wants to take off her necklaces," she said.

"Our brother made them for us," said the one with the red ribbon in her hair.

"He made it from part of a cedar tree," said the girl with the blue ribbon. "He used the knife that belonged to our papa when we had a papa of our very own."

"Felipe remembers our papa and our mother," said the other twin, "but Maria and I were just babies back then." The little girl scooted closer to Maggie.

Maggie reached out to touch the child's dark curls. "You are Rosa, then," she said.

"Rosa in red, Maria in blue," said one of the other girls, and she pointed to the ribbons in the twins' hair.

"Rosa in red, and Maria in blue. I'll remember that." Just then Maggie felt a small rock under her leg. She reached for it and held it up. "Here is our button." She turned toward the red-haired child. "What is your name?"

"Judy."

"Well, Judy, this was your idea. You get to be it first." She gave the rock to the little girl. "Everyone get in a circle, put your hands behind you, and close your eyes." While Judy moved about, deciding who should get the button, Maggie opened her eyes slightly to see the little girls' faces. Each one had a big smile.

When each girl had had a turn with the button, Maggie took them to the front where there was a sidewalk. She borrowed a piece of chalk from a sister and drew the hopscotch diagram. The little girls had never played the game, but they caught on quickly. "You are the funnest to play with," Maria said. She put her arms around Maggie's waist and hugged.

"I know your brother," she said to the twins. "He comes almost every day to work in my mama's garden."

"Is he your *amigo*?" Rosa asked.

"I do not know what *amigo* means," said Maggie.

"It means friend in Mexico," said Rosa. "Felipe wants us to know Mexican words."

Maggie looked down at the chalk in her hand. She swallowed hard. "Yes," she said. "Your brother is my *amigo*." She would make it true, she decided. After all, she told herself, it was not Felipe's fault that Papa liked boys better than he did girls.

The next day, she smiled at Felipe when she took his lunch to him, and he smiled back. But her friendly feelings did not last long.

That very evening she changed her mind. She had hoped Papa would take her to the beach, but he said no. "I don't want to leave your mother alone," he explained. "She doesn't feel well this evening."

"I understand," Maggie said. She hoped maybe Papa would talk to her then about the baby, but he only turned away to read his newspaper. Maggie took Bonnie and went up to her room.

Later Maggie came down the back stairs. She had planned to go into her mother's room to keep her company, but she heard the sound of voices outside the kitchen screen door. She moved quietly to look out into the evening shadows. Papa sat on the steps with Felipe. They both held knives, and they both worked at wood. Just as Maggie got near the door, she heard Felipe laugh. Papa reached out and mussed Felipe's hair.

She wanted to scream at them both. Papa must have known Felipe would come for a lesson. That was why he would not take Maggie to the ocean. She put her hand over her mouth to stop the sound of the sob that grew inside her. She tiptoed back through the kitchen, then ran up the stairs. Bonnie followed her.

In her room, Maggie knelt on the floor. She put her arms around Bonnie, and she cried. Her friends were away, Mama was too tired to pay attention to her, and Papa was too busy with Felipe. No one loved her except Bonnie. She stayed in her room, went to bed early, and cried until she went to sleep.

TWO

THE SUMMER WORE ON, and finally September came. School would start in three weeks. Beth and Harriet both came home from their trips. Papa did take all three girls to the beach one evening. Mama felt too tired to go, but she hemmed the long legs on Maggie's new bathing suit. "Now don't be pressing your papa to go early," Mama said. "There's no way to cover your face. A lady must never bathe while the sun shines." She touched Maggie's cheek. "You must consider your complexion, dear."

The sea was wonderfully cool after the hot day. The girls ran into the shallow water, splashing and laughing until they had to swim. Bonnie, on her leash, stayed on the shore, watching. She looked from one girl to the other as if counting them. When a girl went under water for even a second, Bonnie barked until the swimmer reappeared.

Papa, too, mostly stayed out of the water. "Come on in and swim," Maggie shouted after a while.

"The water's great, Mr. McKenna," called Beth.

"I'm coming," Papa answered, but he did not move until Maggie waded back to pull at his hand. Even then, he swam only for a few minutes.

He's worried, Maggie thought, and she was not surprised when Papa announced it was time to go. "I know you girls would like to stay longer," he told Maggie, "but I'd like to get home to your mother."

"Is she worse, you think?" Waiting for his answer, Maggie held her breath.

"Not exactly." Papa put his arms across her wet shoulder. "I need to tell you something. I'm taking your mother to Houston tomorrow to see a special doctor."

"Why?"

"Just to make sure she's all right." Papa put his hand on her head.

"How long will you be gone?"

Papa patted her head. "Most likely we'll be back before bedtime. In any case, there's nothing for you to worry about."

Maggie did worry, though. She worried so much that she hardly noticed the group of children who came down to the beach from the orphanage. Felipe was with them. "Hello, Mr. McKenna," he called.

Maggie hated the way her father's face broke into a big smile. "Hello there, Felipe. Fine night for a swim. Enjoy yourself."

"That boy gets on my nerves," Maggie whispered to Harriet, and she made up her mind to make no more attempts to be friendly with Felipe. She did not need him, she thought, for an *amigo*. Felipe would be starting school soon too. Then she would not have to see him as much. But Maggie did not know that the wish she had pretended to make on her birthday about school not starting on time would come true.

On the next morning, the one before the storm, Maggie woke just as light came into her room from the east window. Papa had come into her room then too, and he stood looking down at her in the dim light. "I did not mean to wake you," Papa said. "I only wanted to see my girl before we left."

Maggie sat up. She wished Papa would hug her, but he did not. "I'll let Bonnie out," he said. At the mention of her name, Bonnie rose from her place on the floor beside the bed.

"Good-bye, Papa," Maggie said.

"You go back to sleep now," Papa said. "When you wake, Daphne will fix your breakfast. Myra will be with you, of course, and I will call you from Houston."

He was gone then back into the dark hall. Maggie lay very still and listened. She could hear voices downstairs, Mama's and Papa's and Myra's, but she could not hear what they said. She jumped from her bed and ran to the back window, the one that looked down at the spot where the carriage waited just beyond the fence to take Mama and Papa to the train station.

Before long, she saw them. Papa moving down the back

walkway. He carried Mama in his arms. Maggie sucked in her breath. Mama had not seemed that weak last night when she had kissed Maggie. "This is good night and good-bye," she had said. "I'll tell you good-bye tonight, so you won't have to come downstairs so early."

Maggie had put her arms around her mother and hugged her tightly. "Don't you fret one bit, darling," Mama had said. "Your papa and I will be back before you have time to miss us, and I think this doctor will help me feel better."

But looking out the window that morning, Maggie had plenty to fret about. Mama had to be carried. Myra came from behind Papa and scurried to open the gate for him. Myra did not usually move so fast. "She's worried too," Maggie said aloud.

She stood up so that she could get a glimpse of the carriage. It moved down the street, and Maggie couldn't see much more than Papa's hat and the carriage cover. She stayed on her window seat for a long time.

She stared at the back garden, all full of Mama's roses. Mama loved her roses more than almost anything. When she comes home, Maggie thought, I'll have bouquets of roses waiting for her in the parlor. What if Mama did not come home this evening? What if she stayed in Houston until the baby came? Maggie wondered how long that would be. She went over to her desk and picked up a small calendar with kittens on it. She took her finger and found today, Friday, September 7. There was the rest of September, all of October, and November before December.

She went back to the window seat. Then she stared down at her birthday ring. "I didn't mean that awful wish," she whispered to herself.

Maggie slid off the window seat and went back to bed. She wished Bonnie would come back upstairs to lie beside her bed, but she was all alone. Sobs rose in her chest, and once more she cried until she fell asleep.

Daphne, the new cook, woke her by pounding on her door. "You figuring on breakfast, you better get yourself downstairs I ain't planning to be cooking breakfast in the afternoon."

Just then the clock in the hall started, and Maggie counted ten chimes. How could she have slept so late? She threw back the sheet and jumped out of bed to race downstairs. Myra was sitting at the dining room table polishing silverware. "You'd better go on in and tell her what you want, kitten," she said. "She's riled because I sent her up to wake you. My knee's aching me again."

"Did Papa call?" Maggie asked Myra, even though she knew it was too soon for a phone call from Houston.

"Not yet, kitten." Myra put down the silver and held her arms out to Maggie, who went to her and leaned her head down against hers. Myra did not think Maggie was too young to know about the baby, and when they were alone, Myra talked to her about the coming child. "Don't you worry," Myra said as she hugged Maggie. "Likely it won't be until late afternoon when your papa calls, and likely he will be bringing your mama home tomorrow. Might turn out there's no reason for real concern about your mama," but Maggie remembered how Myra had run to open the gate. "Your papa and mama just want to take real good care of that baby, just like they do you."

Maggie stepped away from Myra's hug, and she turned her head so that Myra couldn't see the tears filling her eyes. Myra would hate me, Maggie thought, if she knew what I wished on my birthday. So would Mama and Papa. I didn't mean it, Maggie shouted inside her head. I didn't mean it, not really!

She wandered through the doors into the kitchen. Daphne was stirring up a cake. "Don't suppose you'd know if the mister and missus are coming home for dinner?" she asked in an unfriendly tone. Daphne was not very old, maybe twenty, but she acted like a grouchy old woman.

Maggie and her friends liked to aggravate her by bringing small creatures they found outside into the kitchen. Daphne had complained to Papa, who had said, "No more creatures in the kitchen." Just before her friends went away on their vacations, the girls had found a small green snake in the back garden.

"Your papa will be so angry," Harriet had said worriedly.

Beth laughed. "He just said not in the *kitchen.*"

"That's right," Maggie agreed. They put the snake in a box, wrapped it nicely, and left it on the back steps with a note that said, "To Daphne from a secret admirer." The girls sat upstairs on the window seat with the window open. Daphne's scream carried well.

The girls hugged each other and giggled so hard that they fell off the window seat. "It's the best thing that's happened all summer," Maggie said.

Later she heard Daphne tell Papa about the gift. "Your Maggie done it. Her and them others," she said, but Papa had never scolded Maggie. Papa, Maggie decided, did not like Daphne much either. He complained often about her cooking.

Mama said Daphne's cooking would improve. "Besides, help is hard to find," she added. "We need to be hiring more, not firing what we have." When Mama felt strong enough, she spent time teaching Daphne things, and she was always sweet as pie in front of Mama.

Now Daphne broke into Maggie's thoughts with a shout. "I asked if you expected your folks home for dinner."

Maggie looked up. "I don't know if they will be back this evening or not. My mama is bad sick."

"Well," Daphne said, "all I heard was that they had to go out real early. Don't nobody ever tell me nothing." She quit stirring and started to pour the cake batter into two pans she had set on the worktable.

When she set down the bowl, Maggie reached for it fast. "Never mind breakfast for me," she said. "I'll just finish this." She grabbed up the spoon, and scooted out fast through the back door into the garden.

"Here, Bonnie," Maggie called. Settling on the porch steps, she ate from the cake batter left in the bowl and called Bonnie between bites. When Bonnie had not come by the time the bowl was clean, Maggie felt worried. Bonnie knew how to push open the gate with her head, but she never wandered far.

Maggie set the bowl down on the porch and walked out toward what had been the stables when Papa kept a horse and carriage. Now he always hired a carriage when he wanted one. Most days he rode the trolley to the bank. Part of the carriage house had been turned into a room for Daphne.

Maggie had just passed the carriage house and pushed open the gate when she saw them. They were walking right up the sidewalk toward her, Felipe and Bonnie, just as if they belonged together. Maggie stood there, amazed. Where had that boy been with her dog? "Come," she shouted, and she stomped toward them.

Bonnie did come, bounding through the sunlight and barking a joyful greeting. Her brown-and-white coat caught the sun and held it. A second before Maggie had felt angry with her, but it wasn't really Bonnie's fault. Felipe had led her away. Felipe wanted her papa, and now he was after her dog.

Maggie bent to stroke her collie, but she kept her eyes on the boy. "Where have you been?" she demanded. "You should never take my dog out of our fence without permission!"

Felipe held up his hand to gesture "wait." He even smiled a little. "Didn't take her anywhere," he said. "She came to meet me. Lots of times she comes to meet me in the mornings. I wonder how she knows when I will come? Today I only stay one hour." He shrugged. "The dog, she likes me."

Maggie stared at him. The knees of his trousers were worn almost through. His shirt was faded too, but he was always clean. He stood straight and tall. Was he lying to her? Maggie looked into his dark eyes and told herself no. Felipe was not a liar. She could have liked him. He really could have been her *amigo*, Maggie admitted to herself, if she had not been so jealous. With a sick feeling, she remembered again the jealous wish she had made on her birthday. Maybe she could do something nice. Maybe she could make up for the selfish wish.

"I'm going over to St. Mary's this afternoon," she said to Felipe. "I want to take some toys to the little girls over there."

"The little girls will be glad," he said, but he didn't sound particularly impressed himself. "It is always good when the rich children give away things to the poor orphans," he said, and he turned away from her to go into the part of the carriage house where the garden tools were kept.

Maggie sighed. Part of her wanted to call after Felipe. Bonnie liked him. Didn't Papa always say dogs could tell good people from bad? She wanted to tell him how pretty she thought the crosses were that he had made for his little sisters. Then she shook her head. There was no use trying to be friends with Felipe.

Maggie took Bonnie up the steps and into the back door. "Where's the bowl?" Daphne demanded.

Maggie went back for the bowl, set it down on the table, and stomped through the kitchen with Bonnie beside her.

"Don't seem to me like a big dog like that with flying hair

and dirty feet ought to be in the house at all, let alone prancing through the kitchen," Daphne complained, but Maggie ignored her. She was going to be good, she told herself. She would even stop fighting with Daphne.

Myra was dusting the parlor. "Your papa rang up," she said, and she pointed to the black telephone on the wall.

Maggie held her breath.

"Doctor wants to keep your mama for a few days, make sure she gets enough food and liquid to stay down." Myra gave Maggie a big smile. "Your papa says we're not to worry. Your mama will be fine. Your papa is staying tonight with your aunt Susan. He'll be home tomorrow for supper."

Maggie wanted to shout for joy, but she stood there smiling. Then she remembered. "Myra," she said, "I'm going to go up to my room and gather up some toys I'd like to take over to the orphanage right after we have lunch."

"Well, isn't that just fine," Myra said. "I think that's just a mighty fine thing for you to do."

Bonnie and Maggie ran up the stairs then. Maggie began to sing, "Casey would waltz with a strawberry blond, and the band played on." Bonnie barked right along with the song.

Upstairs, she went right to the chifforobe that held her toys, mostly dolls she had not really played with in a couple of years. She chose the two prettiest. One had on a soft brown winter coat. On her head she wore a plaid hat, and she held a matching plaid muff to keep her hands warm.

The other one was a baby doll in a long white dress and

a lace bonnet. Maggie felt a little sorry about giving them away. She held each one of them in her arms for a minute, and then she laid them on her bed. "I know just who I'll give you two to," she said. "You're all dusty now, but I'll clean you up. You just wait till Rosa and Maria get you. They'll hug you all the time, and you will never be dusty again."

In a hall cupboard, Maggie found a brown cloth valise, and she put both dolls in it. Then she went to her penny bank, a big pink pig made of glass. In the bottom was a round hole with a cork in it. Maggie pulled the plug, carried the pig upside-down to the valise, and emptied all the pennies into the bag.

Right after lunch, Maggie and Bonnie set off. Maggie talked to her dog during the four-block walk. "We'll stop at Mr. Campbell's store," Maggie said. "He's got the nicest peppermints."

When they got to the store, Maggie hesitated a minute and looked through the big glass with the loaves of bread and cooked hams. "Come on," she said to Bonnie. "Mr. Campbell won't complain about you because he borrows money from Papa down at Mr. Rosenberg's bank." Sometimes Maggie went with Mama when she did the shopping. Mr. Campbell always rushed to get things like salt for Mama, and he showed her the meat before he wrapped it up to make sure she liked how it looked. "I wonder how nice he'd be," Mama told Maggie once, "if he didn't borrow money from your papa."

"Well, well," Mr. Campbell said when Maggie and Bonnie

came in the door, "if it isn't young Miss McKenna and her collie dog." He turned to call into the back of the store where he lived with his family. "Josephine, come out here and see this dog. I do declare she's the finest specimen of a collie I've ever laid eyes on."

Mrs. Campbell came rushing out from the back, wiping her hands on a white apron. "A pure beauty," she said when she saw Bonnie.

"She's got good manners too," Maggie said. "Just watch. Sit, Bonnie." Bonnie dropped to her haunches, and both of the Campbells clapped.

Maggie felt good. She walked over to the counter, took the dolls from the valise, and emptied the pennies onto the countertop. "I want as many peppermints as these pennies will buy." Right away Mr. and Mrs. Campbell started counting, putting the pennies into stacks of ten.

While they counted Maggie walked around the store, looking at bolts of cloth and taking a big whiff of the pickle barrel. She never did like to eat pickles, but she liked the smell of that barrel, all salty and full of vinegar.

"One hundred and five," Mr. Campbell announced. "You can get one hundred and five peppermints for these pennies."

"Good," Maggie said.

Mr. Campbell put the candy into a big paper bag that Maggie put back into the valise with the dolls. "Where you headed?" he asked.

"Taking the trolley over to St. Mary's orphanage."

"Well"—Mr. Campbell leaned against the counter—"don't be going into the water. Folks been here this morning say it's real riled up, and they say the hurricane flag's been raised over at the Levy Building. I reckon we're in for a storm."

"Today?" Maggie looked toward the big glass window in front of the store.

"More likely tomorrow, but still, don't go into that water, I'd say."

Maggie and Bonnie went on their way. When the trolley stopped, they got on through the back door. "Lie down," Maggie whispered to Bonnie before she went up to pay. She hoped the driver wouldn't see the dog. Some of the drivers would let Bonnie ride, but some wouldn't even when Maggie paid the nickel fare for her.

During the ride, Maggie thought about the peppermints. There were, she knew, ninety-three orphans and ten nuns at St. Mary's, one hundred and three people altogether. Maggie looked down at the valise on the seat beside her and decided she should eat the two extra peppermints. Just before she finished the last one, she realized she should have shared with Bonnie. She took the candy from her mouth and held it out to the dog. Bonnie took the peppermint and chewed it happily.

Maggie stood for a while and gazed at the ocean. Bonnie looked at the water too, and she started to whine. "We'll go for a walk down there, girl. I promise, just as soon as I get to see Rosa and Maria." Bonnie's favorite thing about walks by the ocean was the gulls. She liked chasing them. She never really caught one, but she loved making them fly. Today, though, Maggie could see that the water had changed since last night. Mr. Campbell was right about its being riled. The water looked brown, and waves struck the beach with an angry force.

Maggie opened the big gate and went inside the orphanage's yard. No children played about there. "They must be eating late today," she told Bonnie.

She put out her hand to knock, but she stopped. What about Bonnie, could she come in? Just then Maggie heard the big front door open, and she saw Sister Genevieve step out. She was young, and her dark eyes sparkled with fun. Maggie had once heard Felipe tell Papa that Sister Genevieve was his favorite of the ten nuns who worked at the orphanage because she was from Mexico. Maggie liked her best because her voice always sounded a little like she was about to laugh.

"We have company!" Sister Genevieve said, and she opened the door wide for Maggie and Bonnie.

Suddenly Maggie felt shy, and she looked down at her feet. Maybe the sisters wouldn't want her bringing dolls to Rosa and Maria when she didn't have anything for all the other children. "I've got dolls." She held out her bag. "I wanted to give them to Rosa and Maria, and I brought peppermints for everyone."

"Wonderful." Sister Genevieve put out her hand and touched Maggie, who liked the way the sister's fingers felt on her shoulder. Somehow, Sister must have known how Maggie felt, because she hugged Maggie next. It was just about the best hug Maggie had ever had in her life.

Sister Genevieve went back inside to get Maria and Rosa. The little girls came out the door in a great rush, their dark braids bouncing on their heads. Maggie thought about how Mama had told her that the girls had been in the orphanage three years, since they were two. Mama said she couldn't understand why someone hadn't adopted them. Maggie thought Mama would be glad to take them even though they didn't have McKenna blood, but Papa, of course, wanted a boy.

"A surprise!" Maria jumped up and down. Maggie knew it was Maria because she had blue ribbons on her pigtails.

"Sister said you have a surprise for us." Rosa moved as close to Maggie as she could get.

"I do," Maggie said. "I have a surprise in this valise. You sit down," she told them, and she pointed to the first step. "You sit there." The little girls did as Maggie said, but she wasn't ready yet. "Now close your eyes," she told them, "and hold out your arms like this." She took first Rosa's arms and then Maria's, and she arranged them so that they would be able to hold the dolls. "Don't you say a word until Maria gets hers," Maggie said, and she laid the baby doll in Rosa's arms.

Rosa made a little gasping sound, but she didn't say anything until Maggie had put the other doll in her sister's arms. "It's a doll," Maria shouted when she had hers. Both girls opened their eyes.

"You're the most beautiful baby in the world," Rosa whispered to her doll. Then she remembered her manners. "Oh, thank you, Maggie McKenna. Oh, just thank you and thank you."

"Yes," said Maria. "It isn't even Christmas."

Maggie left the two little girls on the steps and went inside to find Sister Genevieve, who supervised the children as they cleaned plates from the dining tables.

Sister Genevieve bent over a table, but when she caught sight of Maggie she straightened her back. There was a big smile on her face. Later, after the storm, Maggie thought often of that smile. Sister Genevieve looked so young and sweet. Maggie wanted to ask her how old she was, but she was afraid that wasn't a proper question for a holy sister, even a very young one.

"I brought peppermints," Maggie said, and she handed her the bag. "There are one hundred three of them."

"Well, now, what a fine treat that is for the children," Sister Genevieve said, "but there are only ninety-three of them. You've brought ten peppermints too many."

"No," Maggie said, "I brought some for the sisters too." She frowned. "The pope doesn't mind if sisters eat peppermints, does he?"

Sister Genevieve laughed. "No, I don't believe His Holiness has spoken against peppermints. Thank you very much."

Three

FELIPE ORTEGA got back to the orphanage before lunch. He ate hurriedly, asked to be excused, and went upstairs to look out the window at the water. For Felipe there were two good things about living at St. Mary's. One was Sister Genevieve. The other was the view of the sea. Felipe loved the sea, even when it raged, as it did today. He also loved the sea when it was as still as blue-green glass. As the oldest boy, he had the privilege of having a bed beside a window on the second floor of the boys' dormitory. In the evening, a blue mist came from the great sea to surround the brick and stone buildings of St. Mary's. For Felipe the mist was the best of all. It was as if the sea had come to him. When the other boys were asleep, he often crept out onto the balcony to sit, his back against the wall. There he would commune with the sea and tell it all his dreams. He spoke aloud to the great water, and he always spoke in Spanish.

Now, looking at the sea, he worried. When he had gone to the McKenna place to work today, he had observed the hurricane warning flag on the Levy Building, and he had felt uneasy ever since. Felipe loved the sea, but he knew it was to be feared at times. This coming storm might be a bad one.

As soon as he had come back from the McKennnas', he had gone out into the kitchen to find Sister Genevieve. The noon meal would be served in half an hour, and Sister always worked in the kitchen before that meal.

"A *tormenta* is coming! I have seen the warning flag," he said.

"My young friend," Sister Genevieve said, "you know I have asked you to speak to me in English." She dropped another peeled potato into the great boiling pot.

"Wasn't that only when others were present?" he asked. He looked around the kitchen. On the other side of the big room another sister worked at frying meat while two girls sliced bread. "No one is listening now."

"Still, I think it is better if we speak English."

Felipe frowned.

"Well," the sister added, "at least most of the time."

"I like Spanish," Felipe said. "I like Mexico."

"I know," Sister Genevieve said softly, and she touched his shoulder, "but we must learn to be happy where we are. Now what is this about a storm?"

"The flag is up, the one that means a hurricane is coming."

Sister Genevieve smiled. "There have been storms before. Sister Vincent was here during the storm of seventy-five. Much damage was done on these grounds. The Greens had just given the land the year before, and their home and other buildings from their estate still stood here. All of the Greens' estate was destroyed, but the children and the sisters of St. Mary's were unharmed. The dormitory building stood strong against the fury of the sea. God will protect St. Mary's."

"It may be so," said the boy, "but I have a bad feeling."

"Perhaps you are being given a message, Felipe." She smiled, and she turned from her work to look closely at him. "But you must remember this. When we pass through the waters, the Holy One of Israel is with us. It is written so."

Felipe smiled back. Sister Genevieve always made him smile, and she had stilled his fear of the storm for a while, but now looking out at the sea, he felt uneasy again. Then he saw Maggie McKenna come up the steps.

Felipe let out a deep sigh, and he forgot about the storm. Maggie troubled him almost as much as a hurricane. At times she was nice to him. Felipe liked her then. On her birthday he had wanted to give her a gift, a likeness of her dog he had carved. When he had tried, though, she had seemed so haughty, and his gift had suddenly seemed very shabby. He had shoved the carving back in his pocket.

Now he noticed that Maggie carried a large valise, and he remembered that she had told him she planned to bring gifts to the orphanage. "Just like St. Nicholas," he said aloud to himself. "Miss My Papa Is So Rich has come to bring gifts to the pitiful little orphans." He started to turn away, but his eyes fell on the dog. Bonnie, oh, sweet Bonnie.

Felipe had often heard from the sisters at St. Mary's about the sin of envy. He did not envy Maggie McKenna for the fine house in which she lived, but he did envy her for having such a wonderful father. Most of all, though, he envied her for her dog. Never had Felipe known so fine an animal.

No, there had been one other dog, not a purebred like Maggie's Bonnie, but still a fine animal. There had been Poco Perro. Felipe closed his eyes and remembered when he was six years old and as happy and free as a jackrabbit. His father stood beside him, strong and tall.

Tata had been to town. He had driven the wagon in to sell milk, but he had walked home, leaving the wagon at the blacksmith shop to be repaired.

Felipe saw his father first, and he walked down the dusty road to meet him. But then he saw the puppy, a brown ball of fur, struggling to keep up with the man's steps. The boy dropped the toy wooden horse he held and ran. "You got me a puppy. Oh, thank you, Tata, thank you."

"No, my son," Tata had said. "I did not choose this little dog. He chose me. Followed me from the village, I think. I only noticed him about a mile back."

"But can we keep him?" Felipe stopped running and whisked up the puppy, holding him against his cheek. "We can keep him, can't we, Tata?"

The puppy licked the boy's face and made him laugh aloud. "Please, Tata."

"Well . . ." Tata stopped walking and looked at his son. "We do not know whose *poco perro* he is. Some other child may be crying now because the puppy does not come when he is called."

"But he loves me," said Felipe. "See how he wags his tail and kisses my face!"

"Yes," his *tata* answered. "He loves you, but he does not belong to you. Tomorrow I will return to the blacksmith shop for our wagon. Then on Sunday when we go to mass, we will take the *poco perro* with us. He is too small to climb out of the wagon. He will wait until mass is over. Then we will go about to find his home."

"How many days until we go to mass?" Felipe had asked.

"Three." Tata had begun to walk again toward the house, where Felipe's mother waited with his baby brother.

"Three days," Felipe whispered to the puppy. "You are mine for three days."

After mass that Sunday, Felipe took the puppy from door to door, asking, "Is this your small dog? Do you know who has lost so fine a *poco perro*?" No one recognized the puppy. With each negative shake of the head, Felipe's hopes grew. Perhaps this little dog had been sent to him from heaven. Did not the priest often speak of gifts from heaven? Maybe this was such a gift.

When at last Tata was satisfied that the puppy had no owner, they had gone home. The name Little Dog stuck. He had been called Poco Perro even after he grew to stand even with Felipe's shoulder and to have a chest broad and strong.

Oh, Poco Perro, thought the boy beside the window. "You too were a fine dog, *mi amigo*. Such a fine dog," he whispered to himself.

When Felipe opened his eyes, he saw his little sisters. They sat with eyes closed on a step, and the girl Maggie was taking dolls from her valise. "No," he muttered. "She'll not be bringing her charity to my little sisters. Let her share her wealth with other poor girls. We don't want her cast-offs." He turned from the window and bolted down the stairs, ready to dash outside, ready to grab the dolls from the hands of his little sisters, but he had not counted on Sister Genevieve, who stood near the door.

She lifted her hand to signal "stop." Felipe stopped, but he kept his hand out to reach for the doorknob. "No, please, my boy, do not interfere. Your sisters are happy."

Felipe scowled. "I do not like charity. I do not want these gifts for my sisters."

Sister Genevieve's dark eyes met Felipe's eyes, dark like her own. The boy felt the stiffness begin to leave his shoulders. He resisted. This time the sister was wrong, but she smiled at him. He fought the edges of his lips to keep his frown.

"You do not like charity?" Sister Genevieve asked in her musical tone.

"No," said the boy.

"But we are the Sisters of Charity here. Do you know what charity means, my young friend?"

Felipe crossed his arms and rested them on his chest. "Yes,

I know. It means giving people things like dolls because you feel sorry for them and think you are better than they are."

Sister Genevieve moved her wimple-covered head slowly to indicate the boy was wrong. "In the days when Our Lord walked upon the earth, charity meant love. We give because we love."

"Maggie McKenna does not love my little sisters!"

"Be kind," the sister said, and she stepped away from the door. "Be kind to your sisters and to the girl who gives to them. Have some charity, my young friend. There is room for charity in your life just as there is room for it in the lives of others."

Felipe hesitated. His way to the door was clear. Sister Genevieve would make no more attempts to stop him. He put out his hand again for the knob, but before he reached it, the door flew open.

Rosa and Maria were there, and their smiles seemed to fill the great hallway. "Look, look!" one of them shouted.

Felipe turned his head, unwilling to see the dolls, but Rosa pulled on his trousers. "Oh, hermano, look what Maggie McKenna gave us."

"Aren't they beautiful?" asked Maria. "Have you ever in your life seen such beautiful dolls?"

"Maggie McKenna is kind. Isn't she kind, Felipe?" Rosa tugged on his trousers again.

"Yes," said Felipe. "They are beautiful dolls. Beautiful dolls indeed. Do you know how to say doll in our language?" he asked. "Say it—*muñeca*. The rich girl gave you pretty *muñecas*."

It was Maria who spoke. "The kind girl gave us pretty *muñecas*," she said.

Felipe looked up to see Sister Genevieve's smile. Then he turned and went back upstairs to watch the sea. Leaning against the windowsill near his bed, he watched the water rage against the shore, and felt the rage build inside him. He had to get out of this place. Yes, Sister Genevieve and the others were kind, but Felipe longed to go to Mexico. He would find his grandparents. His *abuelos*, he corrected himself. No one could keep him from thinking in Spanish. Felipe hated how he had even begun to think in English. When had he started doing that? He had been here in the orphanage speaking English for three years, but when had his thinking changed? If he thought in English, did that mean he could never go back to Mexico?

When Felipe was six, his *familia* had left Mexico and come to this Texas. They had waved good-bye to the *abuelos*. Felipe remembered their sad faces. When they were almost too far away to hear, his *abuelo* had shouted, "Don't forget us, Felipe." He had waved his black hat and shouted again and again, "Don't forget us." Felipe had never forgotten.

He remembered the wagon with the mattress for sleeping. It was on the mattress that he entertained his little brother, Pedro. And Poco Perro had come too, riding beside him and hunting with his father when they stopped for the evening. Poco Perro was good to scare up rabbits from among the sagebrush. Sometimes Felipe would be allowed to go with them, following always behind Tata. "Go, Poco Perro," he would shout when the dog found a rabbit. "Go find our supper."

In a place called west Texas, they had stopped the wagon. "There will be work here," Tata had said, and he did find work in the cotton fields. Felipe's mother had worked too. While Felipe entertained Pedro under a tree, his mother and father had worked in the fields, pulling white balls from plants that grew green from the ground.

The small house where they lived stood in a row with many other small houses like theirs. Other children slept in those houses, but Felipe didn't have a chance to get to know them before Tata had said, "The work is all done. We must move on."

So they were back in the wagon again. Felipe remembered how just as they were about to pull away, a large man had come from the big white house. "The boss man," his *madre* had whispered to him, and Felipe had leaned closer because he had never seen a boss man with big boots and a tall white hat.

"Before you go, Ortega, let's talk about that dog. It's a mighty fine dog," the boss man had said. Tata had taken off his beaten straw hat to listen. The boss man had put out his hand slowly to touch Poco Perro. "My girl . . ." The boss man leaned his head back toward the house, and Felipe saw a child, a girl about his age, standing beside the door. She was blond and her hair hung in curls. "She admires your dog a lot. Do you want to sell him?"

"No," shouted Felipe, and he threw his arms around Poco Perro's neck and held tight.

"Hush, Felipe," his *madre* said.

"Well," said the boss man. "I'll give you twenty dollars."

Felipe tightened his hold around the dog's neck. He had heard his *madre* and *tata* talk of the wages they made for picking cotton in the boss man's field. He knew that twenty dollars was a lot of money, and a terrible fear grew inside him. "No, Tata," he said softly. "Please, no."

"I cannot sell the boy's dog," his father said.

"Suit yourself," said the boss man, and he stepped away from the wagon. Felipe looked back at the girl beside the house. She had wanted his dog. He wanted to shake his fist at her, but he did not. Instead he stroked the great back of Poco Perro.

"You have a valuable dog, it seems," said his *madre.*

Felipe did not speak. He could not speak because his chest and throat felt too full of the tears that had not yet worked their way out of his eyes.

The next year, when Tata worked on a sheep ranch, the twins, Rosa and Maria, were born. The tiny girls looked exactly alike, and their alikeness amazed Felipe, who stood beside the makeshift crib Tata had fashioned, staring down at the babies for hours at a time. "Two," he would often say to his little brother, Pedro, who toddled about unconcerned. "We have two sisters who are the same. The same eyes, the same ears, the same hair. Two little girls just the same all over."

The babies were almost two years old, little Pedro four, and Felipe ten when the sickness came. Felipe worked beside Madre and Tata then, in the great cane fields, chopping grass from the green rows that would grow tall and become food for cattle. It was Madre who became sick first. "I hurt," she told Tata one morning as they ate their breakfast of tortilllas and milk. "I cannot go to the fields today." She leaned against the stove as she spoke. Her face burned red like fire, and her eyes looked like glass.

For four days, Madre stayed on her corner pallet. Felipe tried to care for her while seeing to little Pedro and the just-alike girls. He carried drinks of water to her, and he put wet cloths on her head. Madre kept her eyes closed and she moaned. Felipe knelt beside her, frightened, and tried to determine if Madre was asleep or awake.

On the fourth day, Felipe woke to his father's scream. In the early light, he could see Tata in the corner bending over Madre. Jumping from his bed on the floor, Felipe crossed the room to stand beside Tata. His father pointed at tiny red bumps on Madre's forehead. "The pox," he whispered. "Oh, God in heaven, help us. My son, your *madre* has smallpox."

Tata did not go to the field that day. Felipe was sent for the priest at the small church four miles away. "Tell no one except the *padre* about the smallpox." Tata looked over his shoulder at the door as if someone might be listening there. "These people, the workers and the boss man, they might burn this house with us all in it if they learn we have the pox."

It was a long walk even for a big boy of ten. The dust on the road burned into his feet, and his throat hurt because he had had no drink of water since the evening before. Poco Perro walked beside him. The great dog seemed to know of the trouble. He chased no horny toads, nor did he run at the covey of quail the travelers startled at the side of the road. The boy and the dog kept their eyes straight ahead. The boy's heart beat fast, and he prayed, often repeating Hail Marys aloud to the cactus along his path.

"Padre," he called, when at last he leaned against the door. "Padre, my *madre*, she has the smallpox, and my *tata* says the men may burn our house with us in it. Help us, Padre, please."

The priest was young, and his skin was dark like Felipe's. In all their travels in this west Texas the boy had never seen a priest who had the dark skin and eyes of those from Mexico. Exhausted, he fell into the *padre*'s arms, and he sobbed. While the priest gathered his things, for he was the only doctor willing to attend the poor, the boy ate thick bread with jam, and he drank milk. Half of the bread he carried to Poco Perro, waiting on the outside step. The dog was given fresh water, too, by the the priest's helper. Then the wagon was made ready.

"Sit up here, my son." The priest pointed to the empty portion of the wagon seat beside him.

Felipe shook his head no. "Please, Padre," he said, "I will sit beside my dog," and he settled himself beside Poco Perro on the bed of the wagon.

Before they reached the cabin, little Pedro too was sick,

and he died first. Then Madre. Then Tata. When it was over, the cabin was burned. Felipe was left only with the little exactly alike girls and his dog, Poco Perro.

As time passed, Felipe would remember the days of the smallpox only as a blur. His young mind, unable to take in the horror of it all, had gone gladly into a fog, a fog filled with moans.

FOUR

MAGGIE MCKENNA WOKE from a bad dream on the morning of September 8, feeling lonely. In the dream, Maggie had been lost on a strange, dark street. She had caught sight of her papa ahead of her on the street, but she could never catch up to him. She called and called, but he never seemed to hear her.

For a few minutes, Maggie lay quietly, remembering the dream. She wished she could get out of bed and run downstairs to find her parents at the breakfast table, but Mama was in Houston at the hospital and Papa had not yet come home. "Bonnie," she said softly. The dog was up at once, her front feet on the bed, her thin, sensitive face looking into Maggie's.

The girl stroked Bonnie's head. "We've got each other.

Right, girl? I promised Papa on the telephone that we'd stay home today, but maybe there'll be enough overflow to come onto our street, and Beth is coming here." Maggie got up and put on an old dress, one that she could wear outside to wade in the water she hoped would be in the street.

Downstairs she let Bonnie into the backyard, then found Myra resting on a love seat in the parlor. Beside her on the floor was a feather duster she had dropped. "I just felt too weak to go on," she said. "My mercy, I never even got this room dusted."

"I'll dust, Myra. You rest." Maggie picked up the duster and went to the table by the door to work. "Papa says he's thinking of buying an autombile soon, Myra. Wouldn't that be something? Just think of us riding around Galveston in an automobile. I'll bet automobile rides would make Mama feel better. Myra," Maggie said, "did you hear me?"

Myra did not move, and Maggie tiptoed over to her. What if she was dead? Maggie leaned close. Myra'a chest rose and fell gently. She's alive, Maggie thought, and she crept out of the room. She would let Myra rest, and she would have breakfast. She could finish the dusting later.

"Morning," Daphne said when Maggie pushed open the swinging door into the kitchen, and her tone was almost pleasant. "I've made you oatmeal. You want an egg too?"

"No, thank you." Maggie sat down at the small kitchen table. She would eat in here. Maybe she and Daphne could actually get to be friendly.

"Better eat a big breakfast." Daphne set a bowl of oatmeal on the table. "I ain't planning to do no noontime cooking, your pa not coming in till three and all."

Maggie shrugged. "I'll find something for Myra and me okay." Maggie took a spoonful. The oatmeal tasted scorched.

"That woman's too old and sickly to be kept on, if you ask me."

"Myra will always have a home here." Maggie frowned. It didn't seem likely that she was ever going to like Daphne after all. "Papa said so."

"Well, I'm not planning to take on the housework she can't get done. Cooking is plenty."

"This oatmeal tastes burned." Maggie pushed back the bowl. "Fix me some eggs and ham, please."

Daphne made an unhappy grunt, but she reached into the icebox for an egg and some ham. "Like I said, there ain't going to be no noon cooking done by me."

"I don't think that's a good idea." Maggie tried to make her voice sound firm. "Myra is sick. I want you to make us some soup. There's Felipe too. He's probably out back working already, and he stays later on Saturday. Papa says Felipe's never to leave here hungry." She pushed back her chair. "I'll eat my egg in the dining room." Ordinarily, she carried her dirty dishes to the cabinet, but she left the bowl for Daphne.

Daphne stared at her. "Well," she said with a huff.

Maggie moved to the back window. "Yes, there he is," she said. "There will definitely be three of us at noon. No, I forgot. Beth will probably be here by then, and Harriet will probably come over—that's five. Please have it in the dining room at twelve o'clock." It was the first time she had ever cared about Felipe's being hungry. He did, she knew, usually eat something in the kitchen when he worked through noon, but she had never heard her father say anything about making sure he was fed. She didn't like Felipe much, but she might, she decided, dislike Daphne more.

After her breakfast, she went back into the parlor. Myra was awake now, but still lying on the love seat. "Let me help you to your room," Maggie said.

Myra leaned heavily on her, and Maggie kept her arms around Myra's waist. Her body felt too hot. "Myra," she said as they moved toward the back of the house to the small room across a narrow hall from the kitchen, "you've got fever."

"No, it's just so hot. September it is, and still hot as blazes." Myra had to stop talking to gasp for air.

"I think it's fever. Let me call Dr. Freeman for you." Maggie eased the woman down on the bed. "He could come to look at you."

"No, no. There's nothing for that old fool to do but poke at me and peer at me through his glasses. I just need to rest a bit. That's all."

"I wish Papa or Mama were here. They'd know what to do." She paced to the window. "Myra, do you think we'll have a bad storm?"

"No, kitten." The words were soft, and Maggie went back to the bed to hear. "I went out last night. Went more than once to look at the sky. It was red all right, just at sunset time. The Good Book"—she paused to point at the worn Bible on the table beside her bed—"says red sky at night means good weather the next day, red sky in the morning means trouble. Clouds were white as they could be this morning. No, kitten, we might have a bit of overflow, but that's all."

"I like overflow," Maggie said. "I put on an old dress just in case there's enough to wade in."

"No use to hope, kitten. It won't come this far, kitten. The gulf's never swelled up this high. Reckon there wasn't any use in your papa having this house built up on so high a foundation the way he did. He's a cautious man. Now I know you'd like to wade, but I don't want you going off to play in water with your folks not being to home."

"I won't." She went back to look out the window. "If Felipe doesn't want to work in the rain, he'd better hurry with Mama's flowers. It is sure getting dark out there."

"Felipe," Myra said. "He's such a good boy."

"I've got to go get Bonnie in. You know how she hates storms." Maggie moved toward the door.

"Don't forget to finish the parlor, will you, kitten? I'd hate it bad if anyone should come and find it dusty."

"I'll finish, Myra. Don't you worry about dusting. You just rest." Maggie looked back at Myra, whose eyes were already shut. She stepped quietly from the room and closed the door behind her.

She went outside through the kitchen. Daphne sat at the

table with a cup of tea. "Soup takes a while," Maggie said. "Don't you think you ought to be starting it?"

Daphne took a drink of tea before she spoke. "Don't remember no one saying I was to take my work orders from some snot-nosed young'un."

Maggie stood absolutely still. She could feel the heat of anger rising to her face. "All I know is, Myra is real sick. Mama and Papa would want her to have good food to eat. If you don't know how to make soup, I can show you, I think."

Daphne slammed the teacup on the table. "I never said I wasn't going to make soup, and I never said I didn't know how. You act more like an old wet hen than you do a little girl."

"We like to eat at twelve." Maggie made herself walk, not run, toward the back door. Outside, she saw Bonnie at once, lying near where Felipe worked pulling weeds along the sidewalk.

"Bonnie, come," Maggie called, and Bonnie got up at once. "She's afraid of storms," Maggie said to Felipe. "I think she knows it's about to storm. That's why she's so close to you. She'd get close to anyone she could when a storm is about to come."

Felipe looked up from his work, and he spoke slowly. "I wonder why it is that you are troubled because your dog likes me. She will always like you best because she belongs to you."

"Don't be silly. I'm not troubled." Maggie settled herself on the back step. "What do the sisters say about the storm?"

"They are women of much faith in God. They say that even if the waters wash over us, God will be with us." He shrugged his shoulders. "I think maybe this storm that comes is bigger than any the sisters have seen before."

Maggie leaned forward. "Why do you think that?"

Felipe shrugged again. "I feel it," he said. "I have always loved the sea, but when I look at it now . . ." He paused and shook his head. "When I look at it now, I do not feel love for it. I feel only fear."

"Well, Myra says there was red in the sky last night and just white this morning. That means the storm won't be bad. Besides, my papa will be home this afternoon, and we will be safe in this house. Papa had it built up too high for water to come in even if it did get this far into the city, which it never would." She remembered then her promise to be nice. "If you are afraid, you can just stay here all night. You will be safe here."

Felipe bent over the sidewalk, and he did not look up. "No," he said. "When the rain starts, I go into the house. I will put in my work time cleaning soot from lantern globes. They should be ready in case the electric lights go out when the great storm comes." He paused to look at the sky. "When my work is finished, I will go back to St. Mary's. My little sisters are there."

"Well, I guess that's up to you, but you have to eat some soup first. I'm going in now to help Daphne make it."

Maggie turned then to go back into the house, but she looked up to see the trolley that had just stopped at the corner. A familiar figure climbed off. Beth! Maggie had not expected her for another hour. Maggie waved her hand and shouted. "Hello, Beth, hello."

The day seemed happy again. Beth had come from her home on Broadway. There would certainly be no water at Beth's house, no possibility for overflow, but if they were lucky there might be water here. Maggie left Felipe to his work and ran toward her friend. Beth wore a pretty blue skirt and a middy blouse with a big white sailor collar. She looked very stylish, but Maggie did not say so. She knew Beth cared more about fun than she did about dresses.

"A storm is coming. Myra says there is never water here, but maybe there will be this time. Wouldn't it be fun if we do have overflow in the street? You could put on one of my old dresses, and we could play in the water."

"Oh, I'll just wear this one. Water won't hurt it, but there might not be any water before I have to go home. I can only stay until four. Mama wants me to take the four o'clock trolley home."

But there was water. By midmorning rain fell hard, and water rushed down the street. Maggie and Beth stood beside an upstairs window. "Gosh," said Beth, "do you think that water's from the rain or from overflow?"

"I don't know. Let's go out, and see if we can tell." Maggie was too excited to wait for a response. She turned and started through the door toward the stairs. Beth followed her.

Outside, they went through the gate and out to the curb. Across the street, Harriet came out on her porch. "I'm coming over," she yelled.

Maggie bent down, cupped her hand, and dipped up some water. "What are you fixing to do?" Beth demanded.

"Find out if this water is rain or overflow." Maggie stuck her tongue into the water. "Salt," she said. "It's overflow!"

"From the ocean?" said Harriet, who had come to stand beside them. "Water from the ocean way up here? Isn't that dangerous?"

Maggie laughed. "Goodness no! This is just water for wading. It will never get high enough to bother us." She turned to point toward her house. "Besides, see how high our foundation is? That's why we have so many stairs." Maggie touched Harriet's arm. "You could always come to our house if you needed to."

"Nothing that bad will happen," said Beth. "Let's get our shoes off and wade."

There was a surprise in the water. "Look!" Maggie ran toward a small board that had washed against the curb, where the overflow was several inches deep. On the board were two small frogs. "There are more. Look! Toad frogs everywhere!" Small frogs sat on the curb and on every floating thing. "Why are there so many? What do you suppose it means?" Maggie waded into the water and bent to study one of the little creatures.

"I don't know what it means, but I want to catch some of

them." Beth said. "It would be fun to have pet frogs. We could take them to school next week. There are all sorts of possibilities." Beth and Harriet were in the water then, grabbing at the small green creatures. "Help us!" Beth shouted.

Maggie took a step forward, but she stopped. "I can't. I'm afraid."

"Afraid? Of a toad frog? Maggie McKenna, you weren't afraid of that snake we found. I didn't think you were afraid of anything. I've never heard of a person being afraid of a toad frog!" Beth gathered the top of her skirt and tried to roll the material to shorten it, but the skirt did not stay rolled. "Oh, bother," she said. "That isn't going to work. The skirt will just have to get wet. Now get over here and help me."

Maggie took a step, but stopped. "I'm not afraid of the toad frogs," she said. "Not really. I'm afraid of their jumping. I know that they are going to jump, and that when they do I'll be startled and I'll scream."

"It's okay," said Harriet. "We'll catch one for you."

Beth took her white drawstring purse from her shoulder and handed it to Maggie. "Here, at least you can hold the bag. Harriet and I'll catch the toad frogs and put them in the bag." She lunged then and fell into the water, but she came up laughing and with her hands cupped. "I've got one. Now hold out the bag."

Maggie held the purse out, but her arms were stiff and her face strained. "You'll get lots braver, Maggie. Relax," said Harriet, dropping a little frog inside.

"Yeah," called Beth. "This is going to be fun. We'll take them to school and look at them under the microscope."

Maggie made a face. "I'm not holding them down on any microscope."

"Oh, you'll be over your fear by then. We'll play with them until you aren't afraid of a little jump." Beth lunged for another one.

"Good," said Maggie, and she held out the bag for Beth's contribution. "I forgot to tell you we have to go in and help Daphne make soup. She is really dumb."

"How are we supposed to help?" Harriet asked. "I've never made soup. Have you, Beth?"

Beth smiled. "No, but it sounds like fun."

Maggie smiled too. "Me either, but we will still know more about it than Daphne does. I know you put in carrots and potatoes."

"Oh, good. I think maybe we're going to be experts at soup," said Beth. "Sometimes things like that happen to me. One minute I don't know a thing about a subject. Then presto, I'm an expert." She laughed. For Maggie, there was nothing like Beth's laugh.

The girls moved through the back door and into the kitchen. On the stove steam rose from a big kettle. Beth walked over to peer into it. "Water," she said. "Good. It makes sense to start with water."

"Why the devil are they in my kitchen?" Daphne pointed at Beth and Harriet, but she spoke to Maggie.

"You know Beth and Harriet are my best friends. Beth is

just famous for her soup. She used to make it lots when she came over, and Mama just raved about it."

"Yes." Beth drew herself up to be very tall and spoke to Daphne. "You, my dear, will be my number three assistant. Maggie will be number one because she lives here, and Harriet will be number two."

"Well, I never . . ."

"You have now," said Beth. "Your first job is to chop onions. Four, I'd say. Yes, definitely four."

"Four onions. Seems like too many onions to me," murmured Daphne, but she went to the bin for them.

"Now assistant number one, you peel potatoes. You can peel potatoes, can't you?"

"Well, certainly." Maggie took two big knives from the drawer. She had never peeled potatoes before, but she did not suppose it would be too hard.

Harriet shelled peas, and Beth worked on the carrots. Tears were rolling down Daphne's face, but she had the onions almost chopped before the potatoes were finished. Maggie did not want to get behind. She began leaving the peel on the potatoes, chopping them into hunks and adding them to the pot, skin and all.

Daphne grumbled and made sarcastic remarks about the girls' efforts. "This is going to be good soup," declared Beth. "Just you wait and see!"

"Some salt," said Daphne. "Ain't you ever heard of salt being necessary in all food?"

"Certainly I intend to add salt, my good woman," said

Beth. "But since you seem to be particular about the substance, I'll let you add it."

"Hmmph!" Daphne reached for the salt jar and poured a fair amount into her hand.

"Be careful," said Maggie, and she exchanged grins with Beth and Harriet.

"Very well now," said Beth. "We'll wait until the vegetables are tender. Come, girls, let's take our new friends up to your room."

Daphne whirled around. "What new friends? I ain't feeding no more young'uns."

"Oh, these friends don't eat much," Maggie said. Beth moved to the table and reached for the purse. Maggie saw Beth's hand go to her mouth in surprise.

"What's wrong?" Maggie and Harriet moved to stand beside Beth, but she pulled them through the swinging doors into the dining room.

"The purse," she said. She held up her bag and turned it wrong side out. "They're gone," she said.

"Gone where?" Harriet asked, and she looked around.

Beth shrugged. "Somewhere in the kitchen, I suppose. Come on. We have to find them."

"Be quiet about it," said Maggie. "I don't want Daphne complaining to Papa when he comes home that I've brought wild creatures into the house again."

Harriet pushed the kitchen door open just enough to peek through. "She's busy stirring up corn bread."

"She'll notice us more if we just move around quietly."

Beth stepped in front of her friends. "We'd better keep up a chatter, act natural."

"Sure, act natural while we search the kitchen for toad frogs." Maggie shook her head and followed the others into the kitchen.

Daphne stood at the cook table, adding ingredients to a bowl.

"Well," said Beth as she moved around the small eating table. "What do you think of the storm they say is coming, Maggie?"

"There's water in the street, almost up to our fence." Maggie moved toward the cookstove. "Did I tell you that, Daphne? There really is water almost up to the fence."

"Don't know as you did, but I ain't much in the mood for conversation. I got to concentrate on this corn bread."

Just then a frog jumped from the chair beside the table. It jumped high, toward the stove, and Maggie screamed.

"Mercy!" Daphne dropped her big wooden spoon onto the floor. "What's come over you, girl?"

"It's the storm," Beth answered quickly. "Maggie is just awful nervous about the storm, aren't you?" She reached out to jab at Maggie's ribs. Then she moved over toward the stove.

"Yes, yes, the storm. It just makes me scream sometimes." Maggie screamed again.

Beth looked back at Harriet and Maggie. "Did you see it?" she mouthed the words.

"Oh, no. I saw nothing. The thought of the storm just

makes me scream out sometimes, you know." She screamed again.

"Well, a body can't be expected to follow no recipe with you two screaming like wildcats. You get out of the kitchen now. Scoot."

"We'll go soon, I promise," said Beth, "and Maggie won't scream anymore, will you?"

"I'll be quiet. Besides, we have to stir the soup." Maggie took up a big spoon from the stove and began to stir.

"If you want to mess with the soup, get a lid from under the cupboard," said Daphne. "I was just figuring that likely we ought to add a lid."

"Yikes," screamed Maggie. She clamped her hand over her mouth and held up the spoon from the soup. "I'm sorry," she said. "The storm just unnerves me so, and all those toad frogs. Why are there so many frogs outside? I wouldn't be too surprised to see one in the soup!" She looked at Beth and Harriet and nodded her head.

Daphne had turned back to her recipe. Beth went to Maggie, put her hand up to Maggie's ear, and whispered. "Are you sure?"

Maggie nodded her head.

"Get it out," Beth whispered.

"It's cooked by now. The soup's ruined," Maggie whispered, "but we can't admit it's got a toad frog in it."

"Here." Harriet took the spoon from Maggie. "Let me stir awhile."

"No." Daphne poured her batter into a pan. "I've got to

have me some peace while I watch this corn bread. You girls just get out of this kitchen, or I intend to do some strong complaining to the boss man when he comes in. I never said I was no nursemaid." She reached out for the spoon. "I'll tend to this soup." She bent down under the cupboard and came up with a lid, which she put on the soup pot.

The girls stared at each other. Then Maggie shrugged and led her friends from the kitchen.

Just as they were about to step through the swinging doors, Beth stopped and bent low. She pulled on Maggie's and Harriet's skirts. There beside the table leg was a small brown frog.

Harriet gathered him into her hands. "Oh, you poor thing," she murmured to the creature, holding it near her face. "Your brother is boiled with the onions. Can you ever forgive us?"

"Let's put him out," said Beth. "I don't want to play with him anymore."

"What are we going to do about the soup?" Harriet whispered. "We don't have to eat it, do we?"

"Of course we can't eat it, but we'll have to pretend we are. In fact, we'll have to beg to have the first bowls, dip them up ourselves," said Maggie.

"It's a challenge," said Beth. "We've got to get that toad frog into one of our bowls. Then we'll just sort of lose our appetite or something."

"That won't be hard to act out. My stomach feels weak

already," said Harriet. "Just think, cooked frog, and it wasn't even washed."

The girls leaned against the wall in the dining room. "Well," said Maggie, "let's get the survivor back to the rest of his family. Someone has to tell the others about how bravely their brother dived into the soup."

Beth laughed. "Let's take him outside."

The girls sat down on the steps, and Harriet put the little toad frog on the step between her and Beth. He did not move. "Look," she said, "he doesn't want to leave us."

"Gosh," said Beth. She pointed toward the front gate. "Look at all this little guy's relatives. There are even more." Dozens of frogs lined the sidewalk near the overflow in the street. "I'll bet they came for the funeral," and she laughed.

"Let's wade," said Maggie, but just then the frog jumped. "Yikes," she screamed. "He startled me."

For a while the girls waded. Then they sat down on the curb to watch the water rise. Harriet picked up a board that floated near her leg. "I've been thinking about something." There was a very serious sound in her voice, and Maggie and Beth grew quiet. Harriet pulled in her breath. "I've been thinking that maybe I will be a nun someday."

"A nun?" Beth jumped up. "Are you serious?"

"Let her talk." Maggie reached up and pulled Beth back to the curb.

"Well, that's just about all." Harriet smiled. "I'd like to help people."

"Like the sisters at St. Mary's help the orphans," Maggie said. "It would feel good."

"Yeah," said Beth, "but you could never get married or have kids or drive a motorcar."

"Are you sure about the motorcar?" Maggie asked. "Why couldn't a sister drive an automobile?"

"Well," said Harriet, "it doesn't matter about the motorcar. I never thought about driving one anyway."

"I have," said Beth. "That's something I really want to do."

Maggie gasped. "Wait a minute." She reached out to grab Harriet's arm. "What about our pledge? You know, about how we three will always be best friends and live near each other and come to dinner at each other's houses?"

"Well," said Harriet, "if nuns can't have best friends, maybe I won't be one." She pushed back a piece of dark hair that had fallen across her face. "But I might have to break my promise." Her voice grew soft. "I might have to be a nun. I might just have to."

For a few minutes the girls were quiet. Then Beth stood up. "Well," she said, "we might get separated someday, but that won't happen for a long time."

"No," said Maggie, "not for a very long time." She stood up too. Beth and Maggie each put out a hand to pull Harriet up to stand beside them.

For a time the girls waded in the water and talked about the opening of school. Then Maggie stepped up on the curb. "It's time for us to go eat toad frog soup."

Daphne was taking the corn bread from the oven just as the girls came into the kitchen.

"Oh, it looks wonderful," said Beth.

Maggie couldn't say that she thought so. Corn bread wasn't supposed to be black on top, but she didn't disagree out loud. "Well, you can give Beth mine," she said. "Corn bread doesn't agree with me. It gives me indigestion."

"I had an uncle with the same problem—Zeb, his name was. Well, when Aunt Virginia made corn bread, he just couldn't keep from eating it anyway. Why, sometimes he'd have to spend the whole day right in the toilet. Couldn't none of the rest of the family go at all."

"Maybe we could talk about something else," Maggie said.

Daphne seemed in a friendly mood now. She shrugged. "Well, suit yourself, but something pretty interesting happened to Uncle Zeb that day."

Beth looked ready to ask what, but Harriet interrupted her. "Let's get some soup, Beth. I'm just about starved, aren't you?"

"Sure am," said Beth. "Playing in all that water made me awful hungry."

"It was probably seeing all those toad frogs." Maggie put her hand over her mouth to cover her laugh.

"Well, I never heard of toad frogs increasing the appetite. Now, I have heard of them causing warts if they pee on you. See, I had this cousin. Alma was her name, and she was just about covered with warts!" Daphne cut the corn bread.

"Really?" Beth moved closer to Daphne, but Maggie pulled her back.

"Not now, Daphne. Remember Mother's discussion with you about what is appropriate to talk about while people are getting ready to eat?"

Daphne shrugged her shoulders. "Well," she said in a sullen voice, "it did sure enough happen."

"I'm sure your cousin's warts were fascinating, but we're too hungry for stories now. I'll get some bowls." Maggie went to the cupboard.

"I thought you was real concerned about the boy and the old lady getting to eat. Aren't you going to call them?" Daphne stood with her hand on her hip.

"Felipe is cleaning the tools or something. He won't eat until he's finished, and Myra's still asleep. We just can't wait," said Maggie.

"That's right. Can't wait." Harriet moved to the stove, but her face did not look eager.

"You want I should dip it up?" Daphne asked.

"Oh, my, no." Maggie grabbed up the ladle. "You've done enough. Maybe you should go lie down for a while."

Daphne almost smiled. "I am pretty tuckered out, but I reckon I'm hungry too. Maybe I'll just have me a bowl of that soup. Might give me a pick-me-up." She went to the cupboard.

Beth mouthed the word *hurry*.

Maggie stirrred with the big ladle. "I can't find it," she whispered. "It must have cooked away."

"I heard that," said Daphne. "Everyone in my family has real powerful hearing. There ain't no use in whispering. Besides, that's what is supposed to happen to things in soup. They is supposed to cook to pieces."

"I'm not really hungry anymore. I feel sort of sick." Maggie turned back to the small table to set down her bowl. Just then a frog jumped from the table onto the windowsill. "Yikes," she screamed.

"Oh, he's alive." Beth lunged for the frog and caught him between her hands.

Harriet went over to peep between Beth's fingers. "Isn't he beautiful?"

Maggie looked too. "That's the prettiest frog I ever did see," said Maggie. "He's so pretty, I just got my appetite back." She held out her bowl to Daphne. "Fill her up."

"I will not." Daphne turned her back. "Not till that creature's outside. I spend all morning slaving over making this wonderful soup, and you girls go and bring in critters from the outside. Don't try to claim you didn't. You can bet the mister is going to hear about this too. I don't know as I can stay at this job with wild things like you around. I'm going out to my room for a fresh apron. You made me spill soup all over this one. I've got no time to mess with the likes of you. I'm planning to make a cake before the mister gets home."

When the door closed behind Daphne, the girls burst into laughter. "She worked all morning! She didn't have any idea how to make soup!" Beth shook her head.

"I'm really tired of her attitude!" Maggie looked down at the frog. "I'd like to put this little fellow in her bed."

"No," said Harriet. "She'd hit him with a shoe."

"We need a bigger critter," said Beth. "I wish we had a skunk or something."

"Well, I'll fill our bowls while you let our little friend go."

The soup was good. "It must have been a potato chunk with the skin on that I saw," said Maggie. When they finished eating, they made a cup of tea for Myra and carried it with some soup to her room.

Beth set the tea on the bedside table and Maggie, holding the tray with the soup, sat beside Myra.

"Wake up," Maggie said softly, and the woman's eyes opened. "We've brought you soup and tea."

"You're a sweet kitten, but just water. All I need is water."

"I'll get it." Harriet hurried from the room.

"Let me call the doctor for you, Myra," said Maggie. "I think I'd better."

"No." Myra put our her hands and struggled to push herself up in the bed.

Maggie set the tray down on the floor. "Let me help you." She squeezed behind the bedstead, put her hands under Myra's arms, and pulled up while Beth lifted with her hands on Maggie's waist.

"There," Myra said when she was sitting up. "See, I am better. I do believe I'll have some of that soup." She took the spoon and with a shaking hand she guided the spoon to her mouth. "Delicious. Did that daffy girl make this?"

Maggie laughed. "Daffy Daphne. That's pretty good. We helped her."

Harriet came back into the room with a glass of water. "We almost lost our pet toad frog in the soup."

Myra smiled and took another spoonful to her mouth. After two more bites she put the spoon back into the bowl. "Later," she said. "That's enough for now, but I'll have more later. I'm feeling better, really I am. I'll be my old self come evening. This is just one of my spells." She lowered herself back onto the bed.

"If you aren't better by suppertime, Papa will call the doctor for sure, no matter what you say." Maggie took the tray away. "You rest, Myra. We'll be back soon."

"I'm worried," Maggie said when they were out of the room. "But Papa will be here by dinnertime." What they saw out the side window made Maggie forget about being worried.

"It's a horse," Beth yelled. "Right there in your side garden. Isn't it beautiful?" The horse stood just inside the gate that had blown open. He held his head high, and the raindrops fell onto the spots on his gray back. "He's a dapple gray. That's what they call horses like him."

"Let's go out and try to pet him." Maggie moved toward the door.

"You're a strange girl, Maggie McKenna," said Harriet. "Little frogs scare you, but big horses don't."

"Frogs only scare me when they jump. Horses don't jump from place to place."

Just then the girls heard Daphne come into the kitchen muttering something to herself. "Okay," said Maggie. "That settles it. Let's go try to pet the horse. I sure don't want to see Daphne for a while."

"Take it slow," Harriet said when they had rounded the corner of the house. "If we scare him, he might run back out of the gate."

"Nice Gray Boy," Beth said, and she held out her hand. "Look, he has on a bridle."

The horse turned his beautiful head in the girls' direction. "I wish we had something to feed him," Beth whispered.

"There are some apples in the kitchen. I'll get him one in a minute. We need to get that gate shut." Maggie stepped closer to the animal.

"Don't go behind him," said Beth. "I had a cousin who got kicked by a horse."

Harriet laughed softly. "You sound like Daphne."

"Well, she did. Now she does wild things like have lots of husbands, but my mother says getting kicked by a horse didn't cause that. My aunt says it did."

"You go get the apples," Maggie said. "You and Daphne can compare your strange relatives."

The horse took a step then, and the girls stood very still. One more step, and he was close enough to them that an outstretched hand could touch his neck. Maggie moved her hand slowly. Then she was patting him. "Good old boy," she crooned. "Whose pretty horse are you?"

Beth moved to the gate and closed it. "He's our horse now. What are we going to do with him?"

Just then the wind blew open the door to Daphne's room.

Gray Boy turned his head to study the room beside him. Then he made a little snorting sound and moved toward the doorway.

"He wants to visit Daphne," said Harriet softly.

"It's why he came," said Maggie. The girls looked at each other, shrugged their shoulders, and without another word they followed the horse into the room.

FIVE

GRAY BOY went straight to the dresser, bent his head to reach Daphne's straw bonnet, and began to eat.

"Stop that," yelled Maggie, and she rushed to snatch the bonnet away. She held it up, and the girls saw a big hole right in the top. "Daphne will swear we did this on purpose," Maggie groaned.

"Well, it's no good now," said Harriet. "Let the poor horse eat it."

"No." Beth bounced with excitement. "We'll get him apples to eat. Let's put the bonnet on him."

"I don't know." Maggie closed her fingers a little tighter around the hat.

"Come on." Harriet put her hand on the bonnet. "You go get the apples. Beth and I will fix Gray Boy's hat."

Maggie let Harriet take the bonnet. She turned back once

before going out. Beth had a mending basket in one hand. "There should be a pair of scissors in here," she said.

Just then Maggie looked up to see Felipe just outside the door. There was a slight smile on his lips. "What are you doing?" he asked.

"The horse wanted to visit Daphne." She laughed. "He came into the yard and when this door blew open, he came in here."

Felipe laughed too. It was one of the few times Maggie had ever heard him laugh, and she liked the sound. "It was all the horse's idea," she added.

Felipe shook his head. "I need to get oil for the lanterns," he said. He turned to go next door into the stables. "*Niñas locas,*" he said.

When Maggie came into the kitchen, Daphne gave her a piercing look. "Don't come in here if you have critters. I will not put up with much more nonsense."

"Oh, I don't have anything." Maggie held out her hands to show they were empty. "I just came for apples. Beth and I want apples." She reached into the basket and took one in each hand. Then she put the apples back and took the entire basket with her.

"What you going to do with all them apples?" Daphne demanded. "The mister will be here soon. I reckon he'll want to have a talk with you."

"That will be nice. I love to talk to my papa." Maggie let the door slam behind her in the wind.

Gray Boy edged closer to Maggie as soon as he saw the

apples. "You're hungry, aren't you, boy?" She held out an apple, and he took it.

Beth pulled on his bridle. "You can have more," she promised. "As soon as we get you dressed, you can have another one."

The horse chewed the second apple more slowly. Harriet moved to the small dressing table, picked up a white shawl, and held it out to Maggie. "How do you think this will look on Gray Boy?"

"Better than it could ever look on Daphne. I'm really tired of her and her threats." Maggie took the shawl and draped it over the horse's front shoulders, tying it nicely under his neck. "Is the bonnet ready?"

"Not quite." Beth worked with the scissors on the straw. "But it will be perfect for him. A hat that can also be dinner in an emergency."

Gray Boy moved closer to Beth and the hat. "I don't know," said Maggie. "He looks like he might want to eat the bonnet instead of wear it. Maybe we'd better give him a couple more apples," and she held one out for him.

"Those scissors are small. Jab harder," Harriet urged.

"We don't have much time." Beth looked toward the door. "Daphne might already have her cake burned by now. She could be coming in here any minute."

Beth jabbed harder. Then she stopped. "No. We have to try it on him," she said. "We've got to mark where to make the next hole."

Gray Boy didn't want to have the bonnet put on him, but

Maggie fed him apples while Beth and Harriet worked with the hat. "Here," Maggie said, "have another apple. Getting beautiful is hard. I know I get tired standing still for the dressmaker, but we just have to be patient."

"There," said Beth, and she took the hat off the horse. "See, right there." She held her hand on the hat. "I measured with my hand. Get the scissors."

"He's adorable," said Maggie when they were finished and the bonnet was tied under Gray Boy's neck. He didn't seem to mind the hat now, just stood contentedly chomping apples.

"I hope the other boy horses don't make fun of him," said Beth. "Do you think they'll call him Sissy?"

"No. They'll all be jealous. They'll be coming over here all the time asking us to fix them up."

Just then the door opened. Felipe stepped inside. "What . . ." He did not finish the sentence, just stared at the horse. "*Locas*," he said, turning to Maggie and shaking his head. "*Niñas muy locas.*" But Maggie noticed that he smiled again.

"Just a little surprise for Daphne," Maggie said.

"I'm going now," said Felipe.

"Don't you want soup? They will have already eaten when you get to St. Mary's."

"No time," he said, and there was no trace left of the smile. "The overflow gets deeper. It will already be hard to reach the orphanage."

"Maybe you should just stay here," Maggie said, but Felipe shook his head.

"My little sisters will be afraid," he said. "They need me when they are afraid."

He was gone then. Maggie went to the open door and looked after him as he moved quickly from sight. "Felipe is worried about the storm," she said. "Everyone says there is nothing to worry about, but he doesn't believe that." A strange feeling came over her then, the first feeling of fear.

"I probably ought to go home too," said Beth. "Maybe I should take the next trolley instead of waiting for the four o'clock one, but I can't go until Daphne sees Gray Boy."

There was not a long wait. Maggie had barely closed the door when it opened again. Daphne let out a piercing scream. "What is this creature doing in my quarters?" she demanded. "I'll not share my room with a horse. My shawl!" she shrieked, and she worked at the knot that held the shawl around Gray Boy's shoulders. "Never mind!" she shouted. "The mister can pay for my shawl and my hat. I'll see to it." She whirled and moved to the door. "I'm leaving," she said. "The mister isn't coming. Called he did and said there weren't to be any more trains on account of the storm. I'm leaving. You three can do for yourself, I reckon."

"Did she quit, you think?" Beth asked. "Will your papa be awful mad at us?"

Maggie stared at the door. She could not even be sure what Beth had said. Her mind could not take in more than

Daphne's words. Papa would not be coming home from Houston tonight. The trains had been canceled because of the storm. What if Felipe was right? What if this storm was going to be worse than anyone thought?

Harriet touched Maggie's arm. "Don't worry. You can come across the street and stay at my house."

Beth put her arm around each of her friends. "You could both come home with me," she said. "My house is too far for water to ever get to."

"I can't. I can't leave Myra alone." Maggie's heart pounded. "We'll be okay. Beth, you go ahead and get the next trolley, or your mother will worry."

"I hate to leave you," Beth said, but she moved to the door. The two other girls and Gray Boy followed her.

Outside, Maggie sucked in her breath with surprise. "The water's so much deeper. Look, it's in the garden now."

"Oh my," said Beth.

They left Gray Boy inside the fence. Harriet said her good-byes. "My father will check on you later," she told Maggie. "I know he will." She ran through the water, then toward her house.

Maggie went to stand with Beth at the trolley stop. Across the street a trolley car heading for the beach stopped. The driver and several people got out.

The girls ran across the street. "Why are you leaving the trolley car here?" Maggie asked.

"Can't go any farther." The driver pointed at the street. "Water's too high. No more trolleys today." He hurried away.

"I'll have to walk home," said Beth. "It's a long way. I'd better get started."

Maggie put out her hand to stop her friend. "No," she said. "Don't walk. Ride Gray Boy. I'll help you get on him. You'll get home lots quicker."

Beth looked across the street at the horse standing in the back garden. "I guess I could. I wish you could come too."

"I'm okay. I've got Myra. Let's get you on Gray Boy." The water in the front of the house was high, almost to the girls' knees, but they waded through it, leading Gray Boy. At the porch, Maggie held the horse while Beth went up the steps. With a little work she got on the horse's back. Maggie led them out the gate and dropped her hand from the bridle.

"'Bye," said Beth, and then she said, "Giddyap."

"'Bye," Maggie shouted, and she waved. Beth glanced back just once. Gray Boy looked funny still wearing the shawl and the straw bonnet, but this time Maggie did not smile. "I'll go in and call the doctor about Myra. He'll come over and tell us what to do." She did not even wipe at her muddy shoes before she went in the front door.

Maggie had left Bonnie inside beside Myra's bed, but the dog came running to her when she came into the house.

The phone was on the wall of the parlor. Maggie pushed a footstool over so that she could reach the mouthpiece without straining on her tiptoes. "Hello," she said, but the operator did not answer. "Hello," she said again, more loudly. "Hello, hello." Then she stared at the telephone. It was dead. "You were working just a few minutes ago," she said into the mouthpiece. "Please work," but no sound came to her ear.

Maggie hung up the phone and moved to the parlor window. Amazed, she realized the water was up to the first step. Thank heavens Papa had built the house up high. The water would never reach the house. Maggie was sure of that, but she still felt afraid. She was alone here with Myra, alone and cut off from the rest of the world. Beside her, Bonnie whined, and Maggie patted the dog's head. "We're together. We'll be all right, won't we, girl?"

S IX

MAGGIE WENT BACK to Myra's room. She washed the lined face with a cool cloth, and Myra opened her eyes. "The dusting," she whispered. "I need to finish the dusting before your father comes home." Myra tried to raise her shoulders from the bed.

"No." Maggie stroked the woman's gray hair. "You rest, Myra. I've already done the dusting. There's not a thing for you to worry about."

"Water," said Myra.

"I'll get you a drink," Maggie said.

"No. I meant water outside. Daphne came in here. She said there's lots of water outside."

"It's okay. Remember how high Papa had this house built up." She reached for the water glass. "But you ought to drink some water now anyway." She slid her arm under

Myra's shoulders and lifted her slightly, then held the glass to her lips.

Bonnie put out her nose to touch Myra's limp hand as it lay on the bed. The dog whined.

"Bonnie," said Myra. "Good girl, Bonnie." Then she closed her eyes again.

Maggie left Myra's room then and made her way through the kitchen. She needed to feed Bonnie. She filled the dish with soup. "I hope you like this, girl." Bonnie ate and Maggie settled on a kitchen chair to wait. It was then she heard the voice. "*Tormenta! Tormenta!*" The sound came from the back garden.

"It's Felipe," Maggie said to Bonnie, and she jumped from her chair. "Felipe's come back!"

Before she was all the way out the door she saw him. Felipe waded in water almost to his knees, but he managed to move quickly toward the house.

"You're back," Maggie called. "Did you go to St. Mary's?"

"I couldn't." Felipe stopped walking. "The waves and the water!" He wiped his hand across his eyes. "The waves are as big as an elephant's side, like great gray elephants." He took his hand away from his eyes. "Only God can help those at St. Mary's now."

Maggie had to strain to hear his words even though he was near her, almost on the porch steps. The sound of the rain and the wind interfered. "Come inside the house," she called to him.

"No, we must go to high ground. I came to get you. Tell

Myra we must move to higher ground. There is very little time." He pointed down toward the water. "It rises quickly."

"I can't go," Maggie shouted. "Myra is too sick. She can't walk. You go on."

Felipe bit at his lip. "I do not like to leave you." He shook his head. "I did not know before how hard the storm rages."

"We'll be all right. Look at how high this house is."

Felipe shook his head. "The house is made of wood," he said. "It cannot withstand the force. I fear for you."

"No," said Maggie. "We will be all right." She looked down at her dog. "But just in case, maybe you should take Bonnie."

Felipe shook his head again. "The dog would not leave you to go with me through water."

"Wait." Maggie turned back toward the kitchen door. "I'll get her leash."

When she came back out, Felipe stood on the porch. He put out his hand to stroke Bonnie's head. "Are you sure about Bonnie?" he asked.

Maggie nodded quickly, but a tear came from one eye and rolled down her cheek. "I'm sure, absolutely." She put the leash on Bonnie and held the other end out to Felipe. She struggled hard to keep from crying. "Bring her back when the storm is over."

"When the tormenta is over. I'm going now." He began to move down the steps, but he turned and looked back. "God be with you, Maggie McKenna."

Bonnie strained toward Maggie and whined. "Go on, girl," Maggie called. "You go with Felipe." The dog put her paws into the water, and she followed the boy. The water covered her shoulders. Maggie couldn't watch. She turned back into the kitchen, where she leaned against a wall and sobbed. The sound of her crying mixed with the sound of the wind.

After a time, she stopped crying. Maggie drew in a deep breath, took a feather duster from a hook on the wall, and went into the parlor. It was silly, she knew, to worry about dusting with the water rising and the wind sending its awful howling warning, but she had promised Myra. Besides, there was nothing else to do.

She dusted the big mirror that hung above the couch. She dusted the dark wood of the lamp table. She dusted the wedding picture of Mama and Papa that hung above the fireplace. When she dusted Mama's empty vase on the table beside the parlor door, she decided to go out and pick roses. The water would soon be over the bushes. Maggie could not bear to see all her mother's roses destroyed.

She looked down at her dress. It was dry now, but mud-stained. No need to change it until after she picked the flowers. In the hall she sat down on the stairs to take off her shoes and stockings.

From the kitchen, she took a basket and her mother's shears. The wind was stronger, and it pushed against the kitchen door, making it hard for Maggie to open it. When she was on the porch, she almost screamed. The water covered the first two steps. It felt cold to her foot, but she waded to the flowers. One bush with pink flowers was already covered, but three still had roses high enough on the bushes to be rescued.

She slipped the basket over her arm and began to cut. There were red roses on the first bush, yellow on another, and white on the third.

She had only a few more roses to snip when she heard the barking. Whirling, she saw Felipe wading along the water-covered sidewalk. Bonnie swam beside him. "Why are you back?" Maggie shouted.

Felipe shrugged his shoulders. "The dog, she did not want to leave you," he said. "Neither did I." He shrugged again. "Maybe the house, it will stand." He smiled slightly. "I hope so."

Maggie felt like she might cry again. Felipe and Bonnie had come back. She was not alone. She didn't know what to say. "Inside, let's go inside." As she closed the door she looked back. The water covered the third porch step.

"Myra is in her room. This morning she could walk, but now she can't even sit up by herself."

"We should get her upstairs before the water comes in." He looked around the house.

"The water won't get that high. Surely."

"Listen to the wind," said Felipe. "Have you ever heard such a howl, such a sad and awful howl?"

Maggie listened. The wind howled, and the sound made her want to talk, want to block it out. "You must be hungry," she said loudly. "I can heat up the soup. It's good."

"Yes, we should eat," said the boy. "We will need food to make us strong."

Maggie heated the soup, and they each ate a bowl at the kitchen table by the window. While they ate, the water rose. Maggie saw it go up quickly and cover the tall oleander that had beautiful pink blooms last spring. She had to swallow hard to get her soup down. When she could talk she said, "The water goes up so fast." She moved then to the back door. "There's some on the porch now. The water is on the porch!" Her voice got high with fear. Bonnie came to stand beside her, whining.

"Now you believe me, right? We should get Myra up the stairs."

Maggie sank back onto a chair. "Yes, we should get her upstairs, but how can we do that?"

"With a strong blanket. We will put her on it and haul her between us."

Maggie went to a cupboard in the hall. Blankets were stacked there neatly. Myra had put them away when winter ended. Now she was to be carried in one upstairs. Maggie chose a strong quilt and hurried with it back to where Felipe stood in the kitchen.

In Myra's room, they spread the blanket on one side of her bed with part of it hanging off the side. "We're going to move you upstairs," Maggie told her. "Just in case the water gets in here."

"It's that high? High enough to come inside this house?" Myra struggled to sit up.

"Yes." Felipe pressed gently on Myra's shoulder to get her to lie back down. "The water seeps in the back door now."

"You must go," said Myra, and reached to pull at Maggie's arm. "Kitten, I want you to go. Take Bonnie and go with Felipe. Go to higher ground."

"No." Maggie smoothed back the gray hair on Myra's forehead. "We will face the storm together, you, Bonnie, Felipe, and me."

Next they rolled Myra over onto the blanket. Myra made no complaints. With part of the blanket folded over her, Maggie and Felipe lifted her.

"It's a good thing Daphne's cooking has left me thinner," Myra said. "It's not likely you two could have lifted me a few months back."

"Yes, we can do this," said Felipe, but the going was slow. Often they had to lower their load gently and drag her. At the stairs, they discarded the blanket. Maggie steadied Myra on the first step while Felipe got his hands under her arms. Then Maggie lifted the lower part of her body as Felipe pulled. Slowly, one step at a time, they moved up the stairs. Bonnie did not bark, but she sat on each step with Myra, watching.

"She'd like to help," said Myra weakly. "I swear sometimes I think that dog's more human than most folks I know."

When finally they reached the top step, the children rested with Myra leaning between them.

"We'll put her in my room. Over there." Maggie pointed to the left with her head. Together they made one last lift, moving Myra through the hall and into the room. When Myra was deposited on the bed, Maggie let out a triumphant sigh. Then she smiled. Felipe had made almost an identical sound. Then Maggie arranged the pillows under Myra's head. "You're burning up," she said. "I'll go down for water and a cloth."

Felipe followed her into the hall. "The fever." He shook his head. "I am afraid she cannot live and be so hot. My *madre* and *tata*, I mean my mother and my father and my little brother too, they all died with fever."

"I'm sorry about your family, Felipe," Maggie said. There was something else she wanted to say. She bit at her lip. "I'm sorry about the Spanish, too. You can use Spanish whenever you want to, and my papa never said you shouldn't."

He smiled. "I knew your papa did not object. Why do you change your mind?"

"The storm," she said, and she looked down at her feet. "The *tormenta* changes everything."

"Yes," said Felipe. "The *tormenta* changes everything."

They went back to Myra. Maggie got her to drink some water and washed her face. She was asleep even before Maggie took the wet cloth away. "I wish we had a doctor," Maggie whispered to Felipe, who stood on the other side of the bed.

"And a *padre*, a priest," he said. "Maybe we should say a prayer."

They knelt on either side of the bed and joined hands as their prayer joined the howl of the wind. "Hail Mary, full of grace, the Lord is with thee. Blessed art thou among women and blessed is the fruit of thy womb, Jesus—"

The prayer was interrupted by a voice from downstairs: "Hello, the house. Little Maggie? Anyone home?"

"It's our neighbor from across the street, Mr. Henderson, my friend Harriet's father. He will help us."

Maggie rushed down the stairs. Felipe followed. A tall man stood just inside the front hall. Water was up to his knees. "I just made it home," he said. "Harriet said you were here alone. You'd best go with us up to my wife's sister's place. It's further up into town. We ought to be safe if we can get there."

"Thank you, Mr. Henderson, but our Myra's too weak to move. I'll stay here with her. My papa built this house strong. We'll be all right."

Mr. Henderson looked around. "Your papa did build this house strong. Likely the family and I should just stay here with you instead of wading all the way up to my sister-in-law's place, but Mrs. Henderson's awful set on going." He looked around again. "You have an ax?" He looked at Felipe. "Can you use an ax, young fellow?"

"Yes, sir."

"Well, you get the ax right now. You cut you some holes in this floor, make several of them. The water will come in that way, and it will anchor the place. Get you some rope too and take it upstairs with you. Rope's always good to have. I got to go now or the water will be way too high to walk in. Reckon this storm can't last much longer. I'll check on you young ones when we come home." He opened the door then, and a rush of water came in as he went out.

"I'll get the ax and rope," said Felipe. "You go back to Myra."

Before she went back up, Maggie gathered some bread, cheese, and what was left of the apples. She put the food into a basket and climbed the stairs. While Felipe chopped holes in their fine, shiny wood floors, Maggie sat beside the window. She saw the Ketchums, who lived next to Harriet, in the street in front of their house. Mr. Ketchum waded in water to his waist and pushed Mrs. Ketchum and their small son in a wooden bathtub. Maggie pushed the window up. She leaned out the window. Branches of the big oak tree beside the window slapped at her face, but she did not pull her head back. "Good-bye," she shouted. "Good-bye, Ketchums, I'll see you tomorrow."

The Ketchums did not look up, and Maggie realized the wind was too strong. They could not hear her. Myra stirred in the bed. "Kitten," she said, "did you finish the dusting?"

"Yes, Myra," Maggie said. "The dusting is done. Myra, the Ketchums are in the street, and the water is up to Mr. Ketchum's waist. They are leaving because of the water."

"The Ketchums' house is weak. They should come here to this strong house. We are safe here."

"Yes," said Maggie, "we're safe here." But from downstairs she could hear the sound of Felipe's ax. Maggie thought it was a strange sound mixed with sounds of the storm.

"Water is already through the holes," Felipe said when he came back upstairs. "I think it is a good thing your neighbor told us about the floors. We will need an anchor." For a while he paced around the room. Then he went into the hall and out the door to the upstairs balcony.

Maggie followed. The wind sent rain into her body like pieces of metal, but she walked over to stand beside Felipe, who stared off into the distance. "I wish I could see St. Mary's," he said.

"St. Mary's will be safe. It is so big, with great walls. No storm could be stronger than St. Mary's," Maggie said.

"The buildings have withstood other *tormentas*," said Felipe. "Sister Genevieve told me so."

"St. Mary's will stand," said Maggie.

"I hope so," he said. "Oh, I hope so."

Bonnie whined. "She wants to go back in," said Maggie, and they let her in.

For a while they watched people in the water-filled streets, people who would ordinarily be on the trolley. There were men in business suits, women with small children on their backs. They all hurried, and the fear they felt seemed to rise up to the window where Maggie and Felipe watched.

Early in the afternoon, darkness began to come in as if it were evening. A light in the house across the street comforted Maggie. "The Hendersons are still home," she said. "Harriet's father said they would leave. Their house isn't as big as ours, but they are still home."

The wind grew even stronger. Felipe stayed by the window. Maggie took turns sitting beside Myra, getting her a drink and wiping her forehead and walking over to join Felipe at the front window.

She had just lifted Myra's head for a drink of water when a terrible gust of wind hit like a shot from a huge cannon. The glass shook from Maggie's hand and spilled onto the floor. Pieces of plaster flew from the walls. Maggie bent over Myra's bed to protect the woman from flying debris.

"Oh," said Felipe. "The wind, she grows stronger."

"I want to go downstairs," said Maggie. "I want to see what damage was done." Felipe followed her. "Oh," she said softly when they were about halfway down and could see the parlor. Plaster lay all over the room, and as they stood there another gust of wind came. The piano, Mama's beautiful piano, moved from one wall to crash through the opposite wall and then through it into the dining room.

"Mama's beautiful parlor," said Maggie. "It's destroyed."

"More than parlors will be lost in this *tormenta*," said Felipe, and he turned to go back up the stairs.

Maggie made her way down the rest of the stairs, waded into water above her knees, and collected the vase of roses, which had turned over into the water. "Mama's favorite vase," she whispered to herself. "I'll take care of it for her."

Back upstairs, she heard Felipe make a gasping sound. She went to the window. There was just enough light for her to see an object float by. "What is it?" she said, leaning closer to the glass.

"It's a body," said Felipe, and his words sounded strange, as if they came from far away. "It's the body of a child, floating in the water."

"Oh!" Maggie put her hands over her face and a shudder

passed through her body. When she moved her hands the object was gone, swept out of sight. The light from across the street moved. Then she made out figures. The Hendersons were leaving. Mrs. Henderson held the lantern high and held on to her husband with her other arm. The water was almost up to her shoulders. Her husband's shoulders were higher, and upon them sat Harriet.

Maggie watched as the family headed toward the corner. "They're leaving," Maggie said. "The Hendersons are leaving. We've seen them all go now except the Claytons." She pointed to the house next to the Hendersons'. "It's big and strong like ours. The Claytons are still there. See the lantern light."

As they watched a huge piece of slate flew from the roof of the Clayton house. It struck Harriet and her father, knocking them into the water. Mr. Henderson rose and then went back under the water to look for his daughter. Mrs. Henderson held the lantern high, and Maggie could see she was screaming. Over and over she screamed, but the watchers could hear no sound except the terrible wind. Mr. Henderson came up and went back down twice before he came up with Harriet's body.

Maggie wanted to scream and turn away, but she watched in shocked silence. She watched Mr. Henderson press his daughter's body against his own to force water from her lungs. He cradled the girl in his arms while he and his wife worked over her. Then he put Harriet's body over his shoulder, took his wife's arm, and moved on.

"She's dead, don't you think?" said Maggie, and her voice

did not sound familiar to her own ears. "My friend Harriet got killed by that flying slate." Maggie's body began to shake.

Felipe put his hand on Maggie's arm. "She may have been the lucky one, your *amiga*," he whispered. "It may be that the lucky ones are the ones who die first. They will not have to see what horror this storm brings in the night."

Bonnie came to stand on back legs beside Maggie and licked at Maggie's face. "She always tries to comfort me when I'm upset," said Maggie.

"Good dog," said Felipe.

Just then something hit the window, and glass flew across the room. Maggie jumped back, but pieces flew into her forehead. One of them stuck, and Maggie screamed.

Felipe had his hands on the glass almost before the scream was out. "It's okay," he shouted. "I can pull it out. You'll be okay!"

As he gently removed the glass Maggie saw a piece of roof float by, carrying a group of passengers. "Look," she shouted, and she ran to the window. Across the street the piece of roof had struck a pile of debris and stopped on the corner light post. One passenger wore the habit of a nun.

"It's Sister Genevieve," shouted Felipe. "She's got my sisters and other children with her."

Maggie and Felipe took books from the desk and used them to break off the pieces of jagged glass that stuck out from the window frame. They leaned out then and called to the nun.

"Sister! Sister! Here we are."

"It's Felipe! I'll help you."

No one on the makeshift raft turned in their direction. "They can't hear us above the storm," said Felipe. "I've got to go get them."

"How?"

Felipe grabbed the rope from the floor. He went into the hall and wrapped the end of it around the stair posts. Then he came back in and wrapped it around the bed on which Myra slept. "I'm glad we have this," he said. "Mr. Henderson was right about rope." Next he tied the other end of the rope around his waist.

He was back at the window then, crawling out, and moving his feet until he found a footing on the big oak. "Be careful, Felipe," yelled Maggie. "Oh, do be careful." She could not look after he dropped into the water. She turned back to Myra, who was still asleep. "Felipe has gone into the water," she said softly. "God protect him from the terrible water."

When Maggie made herself go back to the window, Felipe was swimming, fighting the strong pull of the seawater. Once he went under, and Maggie closed her eyes, praying. When she looked again, he was back up, his thin body visible in the awful surge. Then he was at the piece of roof, and Sister Genevieve pulled him onto the raft. For a while he rested. Then he stood.

Maggie noticed then that a rope was tied to the sister's waist and that each child was tied to her. The smallest child looked just old enough to stand, and the sister held him in her arms. She put the little boy down. The sister and Felipe pulled on the rope tied to Felipe's waist. Even the children pulled, and slowly the raft began to move across the water, over what had once been a street.

"You're making it," Maggie shouted, although she knew they could not hear her. "You're almost here." They guided the raft toward the oak tree, and when they were near, Maggie could hear their voices in the wind.

"Yay!" a child shouted.

Sister Genevieve added, "Praise God!"

Maggie watched as Felipe took his knife from his pocket, and he cut the baby's rope away from Sister Genevieve. Then, with the little boy in one arm, he began to climb. Once he almost lost his footing, and he swayed with the boy in his arms. Felipe held to the tree and was able to steady himself.

Maggie leaned out the window. She feared that she was too tired, too weak to take the boy from Felipe's grasp and haul him into the window, but when she felt his little upstretched arms in her hands a new strength came to her. She pulled the crying child in and fell back on the floor with him on top of her.

"Bring him to me," Myra said. Maggie had not realized the woman was awake, but she was glad. Taking care of the baby might be just the thing Myra needed to make her feel better. She carried the wet child to the old woman, who made room for him under her covers.

"There," said Maggie, "Myra will hold you. Myra knows just how to hold babies."

Felipe was already coming up the tree again when Maggie got back to the window. This time he pushed one of his little sisters in front of him. "Which one?" called Maggie.

"Maria," the little girl answered. "I'm Maria, and I'm all wet."

This time Maggie knew she could pull the child in. When her hands closed around Maria's little arms, she pulled with confidence until the child's dark hair could be seen in the window. "You've got her," Myra called from her bed.

"I'm cold," said Maria, "and I want my Rosa."

"I'll get you a blanket," Maggie told her, "and Felipe will get your Rosa."

In the hall cupboard, Maggie found another stack of blankets. She filled her arms with them and went back to wrap little Maria in one. "There," she said. "You get warm and watch for Rosa to come in the window."

Rosa was halfway up. "Not so fast, little *hermana*, hold on tight," Felipe called, and he moved to help her.

Maggie knew well now how to reach for the child's upstretched arms, and she pulled Rosa through the window quickly. Rosa stood blinking and looking around the room.

Without a word, Maria stood and held out her arms and the blanket. Rosa went to her sister, and they huddled together. Maggie saw that they were smiling and whispering to each other.

A little boy was next. He had red hair and freckles. Maggie remembered seeing him on her trips to the orphanage. "I can do it by myself," the boy told Felipe, but Felipe stayed with him until Maggie reached him.

"Well, thank you," said the little boy when he was inside the room. "I could have got in myself, but I reckon I thank you for helping." He reached for a blanket from the stack. "Sure can use some heat," he said.

"What's your name?" Maggie asked.

"I'm Mike," he said. "Mike Crosby. I'm eight years old."

"I'm glad to know you, Mike," said Maggie. "My name's Maggie, and this is my house."

"I know your name," said the boy. "You brought us peppermints. Say, do you have any more of them peppermints? I'm awful hungry."

"No, I don't have peppermints, but I'll get you cheese and bread."

"Well," said Mike, "a fellow can't expect too much. I reckon it's enough to get saved from a flood and have something to eat."

Back at the window, Maggie helped another boy inside. He was just a little bigger than Mike. "His name's Jim," Mike told her. "He don't like to talk much."

"You don't have to talk if you don't want to," Maggie told the child, and she got him a blanket.

"You come up now," Maggie heard Felipe call to Sister Genevieve. "I'll help you."

"No," called the sister. "You go in now. I'll follow. You too are one of my charges."

"No, Sister, please," said Felipe, and the nun began to climb. Her habit flapped in the wind. When the sister's face appeared in the light of the lantern, Maggie could see that Sister Genevieve's face was as white as the trim on her wimple.

"God be praised!" the sister called. "All my children are safe. God be praised."

Maggie got a blanket for the sister, who settled in the corner and took a rosary from around her neck. Her lips began to move in prayer.

When Maggie pulled Felipe in from the tree, he fell in a heap just inside the window. Maggie got him a blanket. For a time, he lay panting on the wet floor. Then he sat up, crawled away from the window, and looked at Maggie. "We can survive this *tormenta* together, *mi amiga*," he said.

Maggie brought her blanket and settled on the floor beside him. "Do you think so, Felipe?" she whispered. "Harriet died. So many others are dying. Why would we not die too?"

He shook his head. "No, we will survive." He smiled at Maggie before he lay down to sleep.

Maggie looked around the room. In the bed, Myra and the baby were sleeping. The two little girls and Mike were also asleep. Only Sister Genevieve and the silent Jim were awake. The sister continued to pray.

Maggie thought that she too should rest, but she could not, and she went back to the window, where she stayed even though water was blowing in. For a time there was no noise except the noise of the storm. Maggie listened to the terrible howling wind, to the sound of rain against the house.

Then, out of the silence, the little boy Jim spoke. "My brother was tied to Sister Elizabeth," he said. "They all went under. We saw them all go under, and they never came up."

His voice sounded cold and empty, and Maggie knew the boy moved in that strange dreamworld where he had gone when the real world became too terrible to bear.

She wanted to go to him, to put her arms around him, but something told her he would move away. "Oh," she said. "I'm sorry." It was all she could say.

The little boy didn't say anything else, and Maggie too was quiet. Then she heard the sound of splitting wood and the horrible sounds of screaming. She pushed herself up to the window. Across the street, she saw the dark outline of the Claytons' house. For a moment, it rose from its foundation and floated like a great steamship before it tumbled and fell into the moving water.

"Oh, no," Maggie cried. "The Claytons' house is gone. They are gone too, Mr. and Mrs. Clayton, and their boys, all gone."

Maggie stared into the darkness. "Are you there?" she screamed. "Do you need help?"

"They can't hear you, sweet Maggie," said Sister Genevieve. "Even if anyone lives, they can't hear you. There is nothing we can do now except pray. We can still pray, my child."

Maggie settled back into her blanket. This time she moved away from the window. She tried to pray, but her mind could not find the words. Her body could not stop shaking despite the blanket that covered her. She sat against the wall, shaking and unable to think of what went on around her. The electric lights had long since gone out, but light came from the lantern. Felipe had readied the lanterns because he knew they would be needed. Felipe believed they would survive, and he had called her his friend. She would try to believe her friend.

SEVEN

AFTER A TIME, Sister Genevieve stopped praying. She
went over to where Felipe slept and shook him gently. "Wake
up, my young *amigo*," she said. "We must talk." The boy was
on his feet at once, and Sister Genevieve led him into the
hall. She motioned for Maggie to come too.

"This house, too, will go," the sister said.

Maggie opened her mouth to say that her papa had made
his house strong, but she felt the wall behind her move.
"What can we do, Sister?" she asked.

Sister Genevieve touched her rosary. "We must make the
children ready." She began to untie the rope Felipe had tied
to the stair post. "I will tie them to me again."

Felipe moved to help with the rope. "You take the others,"
he told the sister. "I'll keep Rosa and Maria with me."

Sister Genevieve looked at the boy. "I don't know," she said slowly. "God has put them in my charge." She reached out to push Felipe's dark hair back from his forehead. "You have enough to save yourself."

"No," said the boy, and there was no question in his voice. "The little girls will be with me."

"Very well." Sister Genevieve smiled. "You have proved yourself a man today. I can't question that."

"I'll help Myra," said Maggie. "I can hold on to her while I swim."

Now it was Maggie's hair the sister stroked. "Sweet child," she said. "Your Myra is old, and she is tired. Yes, help her if you can, but do not sacrifice yourself for her. You must live, Maggie McKenna. There is much for you to do in your lifetime. This I know. You must live."

Maggie could say nothing, but she nodded.

"Come," said the sister. "We must make ready."

With his knife, Felipe cut the long rope into three pieces. The sister took the longest. Felipe also took one, but when Maggie reached for one, Sister Genevieve shook her head. "Don't tie Myra to you, child. She could pull you down. Hold her hand, but let it go if need be. Do you hear me, Maggie?"

Again Maggie nodded her head. Back in her room, she helped Sister Genevieve tie the baby to her with enough slack so that she could hold him in her arms. Next they fastened little Mike and Jim to the rope.

Felipe put a rope around his waist and tied each of his little sisters to an end. "Are we going back into water?" asked little Maria. "I don't want to go back into the water."

"Me either," said Rosa. "I like it here in Maggie McKenna's house."

"We are only going into the water if we have to go," said Felipe. "If we have to go into the water, kick your feet and swim. You both know how to swim in the ocean. This is just the ocean, and we must kick and swim together."

When everyone was tied, Maggie bent over Myra's bed. "Give me your hand, Myra," she said. "If the house falls, I will help you."

Myra put up her hand, but she did not take Maggie's hand. "Let me kiss you, kitten," she said. "If the house goes, I will open my mouth and take in the water. There is no use for me to fight, and I will not have you trying to help me. I am ready to meet my maker, little Maggie, but you have a life before you. Remember that Myra wants you to fight hard against the water, and remember to live your life well."

Maggie bent to kiss Myra's cheek, and her tears fell on the woman's cheek. "Maybe the house will stand, Myra," she said softly. "Maybe Papa's house will stand, and tomorrow we will get a doctor for you."

"Maybe," said Myra. "I want to sleep now," she said. "It will be better for me to be asleep if the house goes." She closed her eyes.

With a terrible groan the house shifted. "Stand near the windows," the sister said, "and we will sing."

"We were singing when St. Mary's fell," said little Mike.

Sister Genevieve touched his cheek. "Yes, that we were, my Mike," she said. "We were singing 'Queen of the Waves,' and the sweet Queen did save us, didn't she? Sing, children, sing with all your hearts."

They began to sing then. Maggie did not know the song, but she did her best to join in. When the children came to the part that said, "Help, then, sweet Queen, in our exceeding danger," Maggie closed her eyes.

When the hymn was finished, the children crossed themselves. "We must stay near the windows," said Sister Genevieve. "Come, Maggie, you should not be in the center of the room."

Maggie had time to look back at Myra and to move toward the window. Bonnie stayed beside her. Then she felt the floor rise up in one great heaving movement, and suddenly she was in the water fighting, fighting to rise to the top. She felt a large piece of timber slam into her chest. She wanted to close her eyes and stop fighting, but she heard Sister Genevieve's voice, heard it as plainly as if the sister spoke in her ear. "You must live, Maggie McKenna. There is much for you to do in your lifetime."

Instead of giving up, Maggie grasped hold of the floating timber, and it carried her up. Her head was out of the water then. She called for Myra, and she floated wildly for a time, around and around in circles. "Sister!" she called into the darkness. "Felipe! Is there anyone there? Can anyone hear me?" No answer came, but she felt something against her, something familiar.

Bonnie! Bonnie was swimming beside her. "Good girl," Maggie said. "Good dog." She pulled at Bonnie until the dog was on the timber too, her front legs hanging over it to keep her afloat.

Maggie knew where she was. Somehow, even in the dark, she knew she was still in what had once been the street in front of her house. No buildings stood, but she knew where she was, and she knew the water was carrying the timber toward the sea.

Then, in a flash of lightning, she saw something. Felipe was standing in a pile of debris! He pushed and pulled frantically, trying to free his little sisters, who were caught. Maggie kicked her feet, hoping to make the timber move more quickly toward the pile.

"Maria," he screamed. "Rosa, where are you?" Maggie heard at least one answer, maybe two. She could not be sure. She kicked harder. By the time she reached the pile, Felipe had pulled the rope to where it was tied around one small waist. "Maria," he shouted. "I'll get you free." He clawed frantically at the broken wood that covered most of the little girl. Then he began to work at untying the knot.

"Your knife," Maggie yelled.

"My knife! I forgot." He stuck his hand into his pocket.

"Let it be there," Maggie prayed aloud. The pile kept shifting, and she knew Felipe and his sisters must get away before it shifted to sink them. Then she saw the blade. Even in the dark, she saw the blade and saw Felipe cut the rope from Maria.

By that time little Rosa had worked her way almost to the top of the pile, and her sobbing could be heard. "Let me have Maria," Maggie said. "You get Rosa."

Felipe swung Maria through the air. "Hold on to Maggie's timber," he told her. "You hold on tight."

Maggie moved hand over hand until she was beside the little girl. "We'll be all right," she told her, and she let go of the timber with one hand just long enough to pat the small girl's head.

Felipe was back at work on the pile. Each time he moved a large piece of wood, the entire pile shifted. The current, Maggie knew, could catch the pile anytime and turn it over. Rosa would be trapped beneath. Then she realized the same thing could happen to the timber to which she and Maria clung. "Climb up," she said to the little girl, and Maggie helped her as best she could with one hand. "Climb up and lie down. Wrap your legs and arms around this board. If it turns under, hold your breath and try to scoot around to the side that is out of the water."

"I will," said the little girl, and she scrambled up onto the timber.

"That's right," Maggie said. "You are a very brave girl."

When Maggie looked back at the pile of debris, Felipe had cut Rosa's rope. He pulled her quickly from the pile and had just handed her to Maggie when the debris was struck by a wave. Part of it went down, and Felipe went with it.

Maria and Rosa began to scream. Maggie wanted to scream too. She wanted to close her eyes and scream and scream and scream, but she didn't. She did not say a word. Instead she put her energy into settling Rosa on the timber and into kicking and pushing it away from the sinking debris. Felipe might never come up again. Maggie knew that his body might be trapped in the pile of debris and that he might drown, but she did not have time to scream or to give in to fear. She had to get the little girls away from the trap, from the water that could pull them down too. Holding tight to the timber, she put her feet against what remained of the debris pile and pushed, pushed with every bit of strength left inside her. Then she kicked and kicked, moving away from the trap.

"Good work, Maggie!" It was Felipe's voice behind her, and the little girls cheered.

Maggie took one quick look over her shoulder and could make out Felipe's form swimming toward her. When her legs would no longer move, she rested, and the boy caught up to her.

"You see, we are still alive, *mi amiga*," he said to Maggie. Then he wrapped his arms around the timber and put his head down on it to rest.

Maggie looked back at the pile of debris and realized for the first time that it was what was left of her once beautiful home, but the thought that hurt most was that no one else seemed to be moving around the pile. She knew there was no hope for Myra, but what about Sister Genevieve and the little boys? Were they, too, beneath the pile? Maybe they had some-how floated away. Maybe they, too, were holding on to something in the night. Maggie wanted to call out to the sister, but when she opened her mouth no sound came. All her strength was gone. She, too, put her head against the timber to rest.

"Don't go to sleep," said Felipe. "Don't any of you go to sleep."

The rain began to fall harder, striking the travelers as hard as if little rocks were being pelted against their bodies. "It hurts," said Maria.

"It hurts bad," said Rosa.

Felipe moved to shelter them as best he could with his body, and Maggie maneuvered to be beside him, adding more protection for the little girls.

"Thank you," he said. "We must find something bigger, something we can all get on," and he had hardly said the words when Maggie spotted something.

"Look," she called. Coming toward them was a large door. Maggie and Felipe held to the timber with one hand each, and with the other they grabbed at the door.

"We have it," he shouted.

First they transferred the little girls. Then they pulled Bonnie up too. "You can sleep now," said Felipe when he and Maggie had positioned themselves to shelter Rosa and Maria from the wind and rain with their bodies again.

Maggie put her knees up and rested her head against them. Her body settled to lean against Felipe's. She listened to the sounds around her. Not so far away a woman cried for her child. "David, where are you? Mama is here, sweetheart. David, where are you?"

When lightning flashed Maggie saw the woman, floating in a trunk with another child clutched to her. "David," she cried over and over into the night until suddenly the shouting stopped. Maggie hoped the woman had grown too tired to call out, but she doubted that could have happened. Maggie thought of her own mother. No, the woman would stop calling only if the the trunk had turned over. Only if she, too, were drowned would a mother stop hoping to find her child.

For a long time there was no talk between Felipe and Maggie. Finally his voice broke the silence. "I think we may be going out to sea," he said.

"I wish we could stay in Galveston," Maggie said.

"I think all of our city has been swallowed by the sea," said the boy.

"Jonah was swallowed by a whale, and he lived," said Maggie. "Do you think a whale would be easier to survive than a sea?"

"A whale would be warmer, that I know," said Felipe, and Maggie heard his teeth chattering.

Then Maggie gave voice to what she feared had happened. "Do you think Sister Genevieve and the little boys drowned?"

"Yes," said Felipe. "I think they did, but maybe I am wrong. I hope it is that I am wrong."

"Sister said that I have much to do in my lifetime."

"What is it that you will do, Maggie McKenna?" he asked.

"I don't know what I will do when I am grown up," she answered, "but I know what I will soon do. Soon I will have a little brother, and I will help care for him. I will love him and protect him all my days," she said. "I will love him and protect him just as you do these two little girls."

"These two exactly alike little girls," said Felipe. "I told you that I had a little brother once." The boy spoke softly, and Maggie leaned closer to hear. "His name was Pedro. I had a dog too, a great dog. He was big and strong, and his name was Poco Perro, which means small dog, because he was very small when he first followed my *tata* from the village."

"What happened to Poco Perro after your family died from the fever?"

"They had smallpox. My little brother died first, and then my *madre* and *tata*. The people of the village burned our hut because they feared the sickness. I took the exactly alike babies, and I carried them, one on each hip. I carried them to the *padre*. Poco Perro went with us. The *padre* sent us on a train with a sister who brought us to St. Mary's. The *padre* kept Poco Perro. He told me he would be kind to my dog."

Maggie put out her hand to stroke Bonnie. "After the storm, Bonnie can be your dog too," she said. "We can share my dog."

"Thank you, but if I live, if I live through this storm, I will go back to Mexico. I will find my *abuelos*, and I will try to find Poco Perro. He would be seven years old. Seven years is not too long for a dog to live, is it?"

"No," said Maggie. "My friend has a dog that is ten, but if you go to Mexico, will you take your little sisters?"

"Not at first," he said. "At first I will need to travel alone. I will come back for them." He hesitated for a minute. "Will you take care of them for me, Maggie?"

"I will," she said quickly. "I will watch over them just as I will watch over my little brother."

"How do you know your mother's child will be a boy?" he asked.

"I just know," she answered. "Some things are easier to see when there is nothing but darkness around you."

Felipe did not answer. Instead he began to sing, softly at first, but then his voice grew louder. He sang "Queen of the Waves."

He sings for Sister Genevieve, Maggie thought, and when he came to the part about the morning star, she joined him. Together they sang, "Till in the sky we hail the morning star."

When the song was done, Maggie asked, "What time do you think it is?"

"I don't know," he said. "I have no notion."

Rosa stirred then and sat up. "I lost my doll, Maggie McKenna," she said. "When St. Mary's fell I lost my beautiful doll, and Maria lost hers too."

"Maggie will get you another doll when this storm is over, won't you?" said Felipe.

"Yes," said Maggie. "My papa will build a new house. You can come to live with me, Maria too, and my papa will buy you both pretty dolls, even prettier than the ones you had before."

"You do not have a house now," Maria said.

"My papa will build another house. He will build a stronger house for us to live in," Maggie said.

"Can Felipe live at your new house too?" Rosa asked.

"My papa and mama would be glad to have Felipe too," said Maggie, and their brother said nothing. He would not tell them about Mexico now, Maggie thought. They did not need to worry about his going now. She thought about Mama and Papa. What she said was true. She was sure of it. Papa and Mama both would be glad to have the Ortega children in their home. It would be a very different home. Maggie wondered what had become of Daphne. Mama and Papa would be sad about Myra and about all the others. Maggie felt sad too, but she also felt hopeful. The morning star would come.

Suddenly the wind picked up again, and debris began to fly through the air. Maggie caught hold of a large board. She and Felipe held it behind them, and it acted as a shield from the objects that flew through the air. The board protected them until the streetcar rail came flying through the water. Part of the rail lifted on a wave, and it shot through the door on which the children sat, splitting it into two pieces.

Maggie and Rosa were thrown into the water. Maggie went under, and for a minute she was trapped by debris. Her lungs ached from holding her breath, and her body did not want to fight the water. For a minute, she wanted to give up, but then she felt Bonnie beside her. She reached for the dog's collar, and together the girl and the dog swam to the surface.

Maggie could see Felipe clinging to a piece of wood and holding Maria in his arms. "Rosa?" he shouted. "I can't see Rosa."

Maggie caught a glimpse of the little girl, floating on a mattress nearby. She swam for the child and pulled her off just as the mattress went under. Maggie held Rosa's hand, and the two of them made their way to a wooden bathtub that floated upside-down in the water. Maggie remembered how she had seen Mr. Ketchum pushing his wife and son in a bathtub. Could that have been only a few hours earlier? It seemed so long ago. She wondered if this might be the same bathtub, and she wondered what had become of the Ketchums, and about Mr. and Mrs. Henderson after Harriet's death. Were Harriet's parents still alive? Would they even want to be alive?

Then she did not have time to think of her neighbors or anything as the wind slammed the tub into a large pile of debris. Maggie and Rosa went under again. Maggie could feel the little girl, and she caught her hand.

She grabbed a floating timber, and she held tight to the hand of little Rosa. Both girls had swallowed seawater, and they both threw up. "Hold on," Maggie said when she could talk. "We will hold on to each other, and we will be okay."

The moon shone through the clouds for a moment, and Maggie could see Felipe and Maria. They had found what appeared to be a chicken coop, and they floated on top. The moonlight lasted just long enough for Maggie to spot Bonnie lying on the coop beside Felipe.

The wind came again in a terrible gust, worse than any of the others. Suddenly Rosa was yanked from Maggie's grasp and thrown underwater. Maggie let go of the timber, and she too went under. She spread out her hands and searched for Rosa. Only when she felt like her lungs would burst did she come back up. Again and again she went under the water, but again and again, she had to come to the surface without finding the little girl.

Finally, exhausted, she caught hold of floating porch steps. She clung there panting and crying. Rosa was gone. The wind had ripped her from Maggie's hand. She held her hand in front of her face. Strange how she still felt the little girl's hold. Maggie could still feel Rosa's hand in hers, but Rosa was gone. The storm had stolen her away.

Now Maggie thought seriously about just letting go of the steps. What chance did she have, anyway? So many people had died already. Wouldn't it be easier to let go than to keep fighting, only to be beaten by the storm in the end? If she let go, she would never have to tell Felipe that she had lost Rosa. Sister Genevieve would be in heaven when she got there. Little Rosa would be there too. Maggie's hand could hold Rosa's hand again. Pretty Sister Genevieve would open her arms, and Maggie could rest against her. Rest. Heaven would be a place of perfect rest, but then Maggie heard the words again. "You must live, Maggie McKenna. There is much for you to do in your lifetime."

The words came to her so plainly that for a moment Maggie's exhausted mind believed the sister was beside her.

"Yes, Sister. I will live. I will try." She climbed onto the top of the stairs where she could rest. So tired was she that she was unaware of the chicken coop until it bumped against the steps.

"Maggie," called Felipe. "Maggie, where is Rosa? Do you know what happened to her?" He held out his hand to help her climb onto the coop.

"The wind," she said when she was on the coop. "The wind came and tore Rosa from me." She held out her hand, and touched it with the other. She could not feel her own touch or that of Felipe when he had helped her onto the coop. Her hand still felt Rosa's hand. "I went under the water to look. Over and over I went under, but I could not find her. Rosa is gone. I held her hand, but she is gone."

A deep, sad moan came from Felipe, but he reached out and took Maggie's empty hand.

She collapsed against him, and the sound of their crying mixed with that of little Maria. Bonnie came to her and licked her face.

"Good dog," said Felipe. "She always comforts you when you cry." His voice sounded old and so very, very tired.

Bonnie licked Maggie, and then the dog moved to Felipe and nuzzled against him. Next she went to little Maria, who lay crying in a heap. Bonnie whined and lay down beside the child, pressing close. Bonnie can feel the heartbreak, thought Maggie.

The wind changed suddenly then, and the floating chicken coop changed directions. Maggie knew that they must be going back toward town, back into what had once been a beautiful city. When the wind became calmer and the rain stopped, Felipe spoke. "The storm is over," he said. "I think the *tormenta* is over."

Maggie fell asleep. There was nothing else for her to do. Rosa's hand still seemed to be pressed into hers, but it was not. Felipe would take care of Maria. Maggie slept without dreaming.

Felipe's voice woke her, and he shook her. "The water has gone down," he said. "I can touch the bottom here. Come, we must climb off."

With Bonnie swimming beside her, she followed Felipe, who held little Maria in his arms. They waded in water for a few feet and found themselves in front of a house with a light inside. Maggie watched as Felipe knocked at the door. A man came to open it. "My sisters and I have been in the *tormenta*," he said. "We have been in the *tormenta*, but we came out."

"Come in," said the man, and he took little Maria from Felipe's arms. Maggie followed them into the house.

She realized then that Felipe had said, "My sisters." For one wonderful moment, Maggie thought she had dreamed that little Rosa had been yanked away from her. After all, she could still feel the child's hand. She looked about her wildly, but Rosa was not there.

"Oh, you poor child," said a lady, and she came to put her arm around Maggie. "You poor terrified child. You are safe now."

"But Rosa!" She held her hand out in front of her face and studied it. "I had Rosa by the hand. See, this hand. I held on to her with this hand, but the wind ripped her away."

The woman drew her close. "Poor child," she crooned. "You poor dear child." She took Maggie upstairs, and she put her into a bed. The man put Maria beside her.

Felipe and Bonnie lay down on the floor beside the bed. "Sleep, Maggie," he said. "The *tormenta* is over. We can sleep now."

"But Rosa?" Maggie whispered.

"We have lost much," Felipe answered, "but now we must rest. You did your best for Rosa, and now she is with God. Sleep, *mi hermana*."

When Maggie awoke, sun poured into the room through a window. A beautiful day had come to Galveston, but there was no beauty in the city, only a pile of death and destruction.

For two days, Maggie, Felipe, and Maria stayed with the family named Young. Mrs. Young doctored the children's cuts. Water was hard to come by, but Mrs. Young insisted the children should have enough for baths, and she helped Maggie wash her hair. Maggie had not needed help washing her hair for a long time, but she was glad to have help now.

The Youngs lived on Broadway. Water had come into their house and covered their downstairs, but the family, Mr. and Mrs. Young and their four children, had been safe upstairs. Later, after Papa had come to take Maggie away, she had tried to remember something about Mr. and Mrs. Young's children. Were they boys or girls? How old were they—small like Maria or more nearly Maggie's own size? She had eaten meals at a table with them for two days, had slept in a bed that belonged to at least one of them, but Maggie could not remember the children at all. She could only remember the storm.

Papa came from Houston on a boat because there were no trains left able to run. After a long search, he finally found Maggie with Felipe at the Young's house. He thanked Mr. and Mrs. Young over and over. He shook Mr. Young's hand, and he promised to send things to the children, whose faces and bodies Maggie could not remember.

He took Maggie to her aunt Susan's house in Houston, and he took Felipe and Maria with him. "Of course you and your sister will come," he said to Felipe. "You are part of our family now."

Papa took them away from Galveston, away from the broken piles of buildings, away from the dead bodies that had to be burned with the wood. He took them away from the terrible smell and away from the grieving people who walked about in the streets with eyes that had seen too much death.

Mama came home from the Houston hospital. She sat with Maggie on the porch swing at Aunt Susan's house. "I won't make you talk about the storm," she told Maggie, "but when you are ready, I will listen."

"There is nothing to say," said the girl. "There is nothing to say except that I held Rosa's hand until she was stolen by the wind and the water. Mama, I can still feel her hand. It seems to be still touching mine."

Mama made sad, sympathetic little clucking sounds, and she stroked Maggie's hair. She reached for Maggie's hand, but Maggie pulled it away. Rosa still held her hand.

Papa gave Felipe money for his trip to Mexico. Maggie went with Papa to put him on the train. "I could send a man to find your grandparents," Papa said, but Felipe shook his head. He needed to go himself.

When the train came whistling into the station, Felipe put his hand into his pocket and pulled out his knife. He held it out to Maggie. "I want you to have this," he said. "I want to give it to you because . . ." He shrugged his shoulders. "I want to give you something," he said.

"Thank you," Maggie said. She wanted to say more, but like Felipe she could not think of the words.

In November a letter came from Felipe. He had found his grandparents, but he had not found his dog. He had decided to come back to Galveston and bring his grandparents with him. Felipe wanted to work in Galveston, and he wanted to finish school.

Papa read the letter aloud to everyone, but when he was finished, he handed the letter to Maggie. She took it to her room, and put it on her dresser beside Felipe's knife. Maggie thought that she would give the knife back to Felipe when he returned. Maybe he would carve a dog for her, one that looked like Poco Perro. She thought, too, that she might talk to Papa about finding a puppy for Felipe.

In December, just before the time for the baby, Papa took them all back to Galveston, to a beautiful new home. "Do you mind going back there, sweetheart?" he asked Maggie.

She did not mind. She needed to return to Galveston. Maria played in her own bedroom with new dolls. They were beautiful dolls, more beautiful than the one Maggie had given her, but Maria, too, was sad. Often she would come to Maggie's room at night, crying, and crawl into bed with Maggie. Maggie stroked the little girl's hair as Mama had her own, but she did not hold her hand.

Daphne came back to work in the kitchen. At first, Papa had not wanted her back. "She should not have deserted Maggie in the storm," he said to Mama.

Maggie wanted Daphne back. She wanted something from the old life in the new, and so she protested. "No, what we did made her mad. No one knew how bad things would get."

Daphne often told stories about strange things that had happened to relatives, but she did not tell what had happened to them in the storm. Those stories, thought Maggie, are too real, too big.

Beth, whose house had only water damage to the first floor, wanted Maggie to visit her, but being with Beth made Maggie think about Harriet. For a long time she did not want to see Beth. Then one day Beth came to Maggie's new house.

They sat for a long time on the new porch. At first they did not talk. Finally Maggie wanted to talk. "I saw her die," Maggie said. "I saw that piece of slate hit Harriet, and I saw her go under the water."

"She will never grow up," said Beth. "She will never be a sister."

"I wonder why she died." Maggie ran her hand across the new white porch rail. "I wonder why Harriet died, and I didn't."

"My mother says that we should not question," said Beth.

"I question," said Maggie. "I will always question."

"Remember Gray Boy?" said Beth. "No one ever came for him. My father gave him to a man who needed a horse."

Maggie smiled. "Did he still have the bonnet?"

"No," said Beth. "It blew off before we got home."

"I feel tired now," said Maggie. "Maybe I should go inside and lie down."

"Don't go inside," said Beth. "Don't quit being my friend because Harriet is gone. I don't want to lose two friends." Beth started to cry.

"I won't go inside," said Maggie. "We can be two best friends instead of three. We can still live on the same street when we grow up, but we will always remember Harriet."

A new housekeeper came to take Myra's place. She smiled at Maggie, but Maggie did not offer to help her clean. Nothing was the same in the new house. Still, Maggie thought maybe someday it would seem like home.

A new Galveston was rising from the ruins. Maggie

watched in wonder as sand was piped in to raise the whole city away from the water. New houses were built, new businesses sprang up, and after a time, there was a new wall—a huge wall to keep out the sea.

Galveston had changed, but it was still alive.

Maggie's little brother was born just before Christmas. Mama and Papa were filled with joy. Maggie, too, felt glad. She loved to hold the small boy, who was named Charles after his father. "I'll call him Charlie," Maggie said. When the weather was good, she and Beth pushed little Charlie's carriage on the hard-packed sand along the ocean. She looked at the ocean, and she remembered—remembered the dark water, the deaths, and her determination to live.

Sometimes if Maggie stopped walking for long to look at the sea, little Charlie would stir in his carriage. "Sleep, little brother," she would croon to the baby, and she would move the carriage back and forth. "Sleep to the sound of the sea. The water is terrible, but it is wonderful, too. Someday I will teach you to swim in the sea, and someday, when you are much older, I will tell you what the sea took from Galveston and from me. I will teach you not only to fear the sea but to love it, too."